THE BOOK OF THINGS UNKNOWN

THE BOOK OF THINGS UNKNOWN

VARIATION ON A THEME BY BORGES

BY ANDREI DÎRLĂU

St. Nicholas Press

© Andrei Dîrlău (*The Book of Things Unknown*).
All rights reserved.
First Edition

The Book of Things Unknown is licensed to
St. Nicholas Press/Road to Emmaus Foundation.

This book may not be reproduced in whole or in part
(except copying permitted by US Copyright law
and quotes by reviewers for the public press)
without written permission from the publisher.

St. Nicholas Press is an imprint of the Road to Emmaus Foundation.

Publications may be purchased in quantity for
educational, business or promotional use.
For ordering information write or call:

Road to Emmaus Foundation / St. Nicholas Press
PO Box 198
Maysville, MO 64469

Phone and Fax: (+1) 816-449-5231
Email: stnicholaspress@gmail.com
Visit our website: www.stnicholaspress.net

ISBN: 978-1-63551-104-8
Library of Congress Control Number: 2020949418

Layout and Cover: Bruce Petersen Art Direction & Design

Interior Illustrations: Courtesy of Romanian artist Ecaterina Orbulescu.

"nec tamen consumebatur"[1]
Exodus 3:2

"So much fire, so much gold"
Mihai Eminescu

*Attar of Nishapur
looked at the rose and said: – I'm holding
an imprecise sphere in my hand.*
J. L. Borges, *The Unending Rose*

*"where disparate things acquire a meaning too complex
to be defined, too subtle to become language."*
Ioan Petru Culianu, *The Tibetan Runner*

Tout, au monde, existe pour aboutir à un livre[2]
Stéphane Mallarmé

---

1 "The bush was burning, yet not consumed."
2 "Everything in the world exists in order to end up in a book."

CONTENTS

Chapter 1	The Library	9
Chapter 2	Hypertext	16
Chapter 3	Fanya	21
Chapter 4	Fahrenheit '89	28
Chapter 5	Florigera Rosis Halo	35
Chapter 6	Photini	39
Chapter 7	'Aṭṭār	43
Chapter 8	The Book About the Qilin	48
Chapter 9	Zahir	51
Chapter 10	The Book of Things Unknown	55
Chapter 11	The Book of Things Unintelligible	58
Chapter 12	The Book of Things Invisible	62
Chapter 13	The Book of Things Ignored	65
Chapter 14	*Illuminatio*. The Book of Things Mysterious	69
Epilogue		74
References		78
Notes on Illustration		80

1
THE LIBRARY

Libraries had always fascinated me. Ever since childhood, the huge family library, occupying the top floor of our old ivied house in Acacia Street, had seemed to me a miraculous place, where the square pages of the books that I read on lonely evenings seemed to literally take the shape of the circle of light cast by the golden shade of my bedside lamp, turning globular like Chinese lampions lit from the inside. As a matter of fact, the entire house was full of books, which seemed to proliferate like an organism with a life of its own, a vegetable life like that of a plant thriving on black typo-ink sap. At other times I would see them as a paper sea tide threatening to flood the whole space, overflowing down to the ground floor, and outside into the garden, filling the garage which had found its place among the irises, azalea and honeysuckle under the old nut tree in the front yard. On hot summer nights when, blear-eyed from too much reading, I went out to watch the stars shimmering in the stifling air, it seemed to me that the leathery, glabrous leaves covering the facade gave the house a disquieting air, like a dark pond with a vertical surface, stirred by green waves, in which perhaps its former inhabitants, unknown ancestors of mine, had drowned.

The garage was a strange, oval-shaped construction, hunkered under the huge tree, still green, which produced in autumn some enormous, unusually round nuts. Its warped form had been the only one allowed by the small available space, squeezed as it was between the unlimited tree, the brick wall of the garden, and a derelict, waterless fountain with dilapidated sides of grey travertine, exhibiting a small, square, pyramidal stone tower in the middle, like an unfinished, ash-colored mini-Babel. The modest shelter was made by my parents to lodge a car – a red Dacia 1300 with green upholstery – which they had won with a five-thousand-lei Savings House checkbook with car awards. But they never used it, and a few months later they sold it in order to buy more books and store them in its place.

Even in that minuscule cage, countless full shelves soon appeared, replacing the ephemeral vehicle. The metallic bookstands were of the same type as those inside the house, and were all clad by my mother with zipped, blue dust covers. I always wondered how it was possible that, once I entered the little car shed, space itself seemed to undergo an implausible expansion. The minute ovoid enclosure seemed to become infinite, and I could not understand how the tiny egg of masonry was able to accommodate so many shelves, as if it would inexplicably become dilated. Just like the house itself, in fact, which seemed to me, in my childhood, to have hundreds or thousands of rooms. And in a way it actually did, in the same way in which those palaces of memory, built mentally as imaginary mnemonic contrivances by Simonides and Cicero, and before them, by cultures of primary orality, had thousands of rooms, or other dreamed-up loci, meticulously associated with thousands of remembered pieces of information. Except that, unlike those mental edifices, so fashionable during the Renaissance, which needed to have a fixed structure in order to allow memorized things to be always found, without fail, in the same place, the elusory house where I lived seemed to have an unstable configuration, a fluid architecture of volatile rooms that kept changing their place and their shape, filled with books just as puzzling and elusive. I would get lost, every time, with the secret pleasure of adventure, in always new rooms, baffled by the objective impossibility that they should contain all those countless shelves, which seemed to have been arranged always differently. Neither could I figure who was permuting them so effectively, and no matter how hard I tried, I was never able to remember their ever different arrangement, nor the location of any particular book. In fact, I do not remember having ever been able to find the same book twice, neither in the house, nor in the garage.

But I had nothing to regret: under the blue covers, every time I pulled a zip, I would discover untold wonders, always others: world atlases with colorful maps of all the continents; encyclopedias with illustrations of the most bizarre things imaginable; travel books with pictures of mountains sprinkled with glacial lakes, large rivers winding through luxuriant jungles, stunning waterfalls and endless deserts; treatises on ancient mythologies and world religions, with photographs of pagodas, temples, pyramids, statues of strange gods and people dressed in sumptuous ritual garments; astronomy compendia with images of planets, stars and galaxies, which my mother would patiently explain to me. She was actually the only one who kept a certain order in the domestic chaos, the only one who could easily find her way through the tangle of shelves and volumes spread everywhere, the only one who knew exactly, at any moment, the whereabouts of any book my father happened to ask for, and who brought it to him, smiling like some enigmatic and punctilious Ariadne.

Sometimes, wandering among the bookstands which filled most of the rooms, I wondered what our world would look like, as seen by some hypothetical beings who were to dwell on the other side of books? These beings would be the characters of all the books ever written. How would they see us, looking from another dimension, beginning right behind the volumes strung on their shelves? I imagined the library like a mirror through which one could enter, as through a portal, into another world. This would be a diaphanous universe, governed by its own laws of symmetry, like in Lewis Carroll's book, and populated by bookish creatures with delicate, translucent bodies, made of dream-stuff. To these people, their world would be the real one, while ours – a fictional one, which they saw through a screen made up of multicolored covers, a world in reverse, often absurd (though not more absurd than theirs), whose arrogant inhabitants pretend they were the only real ones, usurping their right to exist. Or perhaps they would be us, projected into a parallel dimension, our virtual doubles, but leading autonomous lives, although reflecting ours. I would then pluck an entire row of books out of their rack, searching in the empty space for evidence of this unseen existence behind libraries. I had the uneasy feeling I was being watched by the invisible eyes of the characters in the books which lay scattered on the carpet; I fancied hearing their beseeching, tender, or furious voices. I imagined they wanted to communicate with me, to convey God knew what secret

messages, of apocalyptic relevance. Using a magnifying glass taken from my father's study, I carefully checked the metal panel at the rear of the stand, looking for the traces of some presence, the signs of a passage, the relics of some secret habitation. Eventually weary, I gave up, placing the books back, but still harboring the inkling that I missed something, that somewhere back there was yet some proof of the tangible reality of the imaginary universe lying "beyond" them.

And so I spent my childhood in the loneliness of that Gutenbergian universe, reigning over an empire of graphemes, but also captive within a paper bunker in which nothing could touch me. Immersed in stories, I looked at the outside world as a succession of almost abstract seasons, which sent me the same signals every year. In winter, the snow-laden branches of the nut-tree bumped against the window of my room on the second floor. I liked the blizzard the most, when angry blasts of wind dashed the curtains of thick flakes over the old houses and the yards of uncertain shape, defying geometry, of the ancient suburb of the Sylvester parish. Somewhere to the right I saw the spires of the Sylvester church and the odd architecture of the belfry, where lived an orphan boy of my age. In spring, woolly-voiced collared doves cooed on the walls like drugged lovers, and in May my street, although named Acacia, was flooded by the fragrance of lime and honeysuckle. In summer I would read outside, in the garden, on a chair by the fountain, where my mother brought me Joffre-cakes, almond tarts, and jam-filled pancakes. In the shade of the nut-tree the heat was bearable, the stuffy restfulness put me to sleep, and I dreamt, all mixed up, characters from the books of my first childhood – the Grimm Brothers, the legends of Mount Olympus, *One Thousand and One Nights*, *The Fairy-tales of Man*, *The Adventures of Little Onion*, *Dunno in Sun City*, later on – Verne, Wells, Twain, London. In autumn, the air turned the color, and almost the thickness, of honey, the sky was turquoise, and the world in the books I read also became mild and nostalgic like the days of late September. School began, yet it always remained only half real. My true reality, the world defining my identity, was still at home, the library-universe in which I grew and which grew along with me. Thus went by the springs and autumns of my childhood, then of my adolescence, in dreamlike succession, like the passing of the springs and autumns of the Kingdom of Lu in the old Chinese chronicle that I was to discover later, with its tales of eclipses and fabulous beasts.

Very early on, I had the intuition that my parents were bound not just by a deep love, visible even in the way they understood each other at a glance, but also in their common passion for books. My father's first name seemed to have apriorically decided his vocation. In fact, he always made jokes on his own name, Homer Palamas, saying it was a quaint antinomic combination, just like himself.[3] He was unexpectedly charming, mildly misanthropic, shockingly erudite, and predictably introverted, yet of a great generosity and warmth. Apart from the fact that he was smoking a pipe, he had surprisingly few quirks. Although the library was for him, too, the perfect definition of a home, he had nothing in common with the maniac sinologist Kien, Canetti's character who dreamt hemorrhages and fires of books. He had won a certain notoriety as a translator from classical languages, and he had even produced a new and rather widely acclaimed, albeit useless, version of *The Odyssey* in Homeric hexametres, ranked along with the previously unsurpassed translation made by Murnu. Unfortunately he died a premature death, from a lung disease that he would call, with bookish humor, "Chloé's water lily," alluding to a novel that had been the pretext under which he had met my mother – in a library, where else? – and which had become a kind of mirrored epitome of their life.

Later on, after his death, my mother showed me some manuscripts which he had no longer been able to publish. Among them there was also a leather-bound stack of typed sheets, still smelling of Troost tobacco, that she took with great care out of a drawer in his desk. It was a translation from Latin of two short treatises by St. Bonaventura on the union with God through contemplation, *The Journey of the Mind into God,* and *The Triple Way: Love Enkindled,* or *The Way of the Mind into Itself.* These titles were going to sink forever into the circular labyrinth of my memory, sublimated in the double archetype of a twin journey which he could no longer undertake, but which I felt he had bequeathed to me like a sort of implicit testament. It was also the last thing my mother spoke to me about; she did not survive long after my father's departure.

Probably that was why I felt that, along with my parent's house, library, and bookmania, I had also inherited, enciphered somewhere in the interregnum of my subconscious, a diffuse sense of mission, no less imperious for being only vaguely intuited. For the subconscious is a no man's land which

---

3 Homer Palamas' name: Homer was a pagan, while St. Gregory Palamas was a Christian saint – hence the antinomy. Homer was blind, while St. Gregory is the theologian of Divine Light, a second antinomy.

pertains to memory, insofar as it can generate recollections, and at the same time it does not, since their surge to the conscious level escapes the control of our will. All that I was dimly aware of was that, in a fuzzy way, it had to do with books, but also with a love prematurely ended.

Admittedly, as the years went by, their image started to become mythicized in my mind. I gradually came to be less sure what was truth and what was fiction created by myself. They had discreetly vanished from my life, leaving me with everything I needed, but without becoming a burden. I started to think of them more and more like some ideal parents, perhaps all too perfect, making an increasingly blurred distinction between those they had really been, and the imaginary ones whom I would have maybe liked to have. Their faces were receding into a legend whose memory, perforce at least partially false, had started to haunt me like some unattainable model.

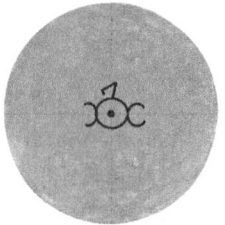

2
HYPERTEXT

I have no intention of weaving a detailed chronicle of those years. It will suffice to resort to a selective evocation of a handful of disparate memories, in search, above all, for constants, symmetries, and repetitions (which are, as we know, approximations of eternity), in order to draw the frame of the events to come – a frame which seems all the more unreal as it is more vaguely outlined. Yet, in this fragmentary sketch, the benevolent reader shall discern the poetry of utterly prosaic times, an unlikely poetry born of evasion and dream.

As it was to be expected, I spent many years in the libraries of Bucharest. My favorite was the splendid Central University Library, the old palace of the Charles I von Hohenzollern Foundation, subsequently burnt to the ground during the Revolution, on the Christmas Eve of 1989, under the pretext that it sheltered "terrorists" (thus I had one more proof of the subversive power of books). Although I was only a university student, then a graduate, I was tolerated there, in the luxuriously decked Professors' Reading Room, with its intricately carved boiserie, through the good will of a pretty, elegant, red-haired, always sad librarian. She had been, apparently, moved by the assiduity of the lonely young man, who would sit there all day long, and who seemed to have set as his impossible goal, like some Wallachian Pécuchet, to read all the books in the library.

Then there was the State Central Library, ignored by everyone under the cryptical acronym "SCL," lying across the street from the National Bank (only much later, in 2010, it was to be moved, under the name of National Library, onto Union Boulevard, into a huge new building whose construction had lasted a quarter of a century, and which bore as a firm, for many years, no one knew why, instead of its own name, an enormous advertising board intermittently blinking *Samsung*). There were also the library of the Faculty of Letters, hosted by the old university building in Edgar Quinet Street, that of the Faculty of Foreign Language and Literature (hidden in the basement of the charming edifice of a former boarding school for girls), the austere philosophy library close to the Opera House, the tiny Municipal Library, and finally the semi-forbidden French, British, and American Libraries, where, back in the 1980's, a mere subscription was tantamount to an act of quasi-dissidence – a fact which obviously made them even more attractive.

They were not many, just an ennead, but enough for me to weave an entire metaphysics around the symbolism of that number. For, after all, doesn't everything, followed through to its conclusion, end up in metaphysics?

*

The silence of libraries would always give me an almost amniotic feeling of safety. In their silent Babel, among their paneled walls, which were but masonry infrastructures of polyglot printed labyrinths (for all true labyrinths are made not of brick or cement, but of words, as all serious readers and librarians invariably find out sooner or later in their career), sheltered by thousands of dusty tomes, I felt protected from the aggressive ubiquitous void of ideology, from the rhynocerized ignorance which could take barbarous forms.

Certainly, it was just a mirage like any other. Because, in reality, what is more precarious than a book – a frail organic artifact, so inflammable, so degradable, so utterly perishable? What can be more fragile than a library? What sort of protection could it provide, when it is unable to protect even itself?

And yet, in those strange eighties – the years of my lonely apprenticeship, spent in a cardboard enclave, as it were, – the mirage of the protection provided by the rickety webs of cellulose would still persist. It is true I was still very young...

A factitious and strangely tenacious illusion made me feel, in the libraries of my youth, in those spaces framed by writing-impregnated pulp, not merely protected, but even *amplified*. I felt my thought expanded, endlessly reverberated by the millions of captive thoughts, linguistically encapsulated and preserved, embalmed in the myrrh of words, within the tiny paper sarcophagi of the countless volumes ranged on the shelves, sequenced by mysterious codes.

In fact, at some point I was even tempted to study library science. I learned a few classification systems used in libraries, and I amused myself for a while inventing a new variation thereof, applying a principle borrowed from John Wilkins' "philosophical language." To create it, I used, apart from the usual numbers and letters, twenty-two of the simplest radicals which compose the Chinese ideograms, twenty-two astrological symbols, and the letters of the Hebrew alphabet. (I have forgotten that absurd code; I only remember that, for some obscure reason, I had assigned to God the sequence: *Aleph*– the *Wang* ideogram – the Sun symbol.)

However, I soon became bored of that exercise: I found the idea of an infinite maze of books far more attractive than that of a banal enclosure, ordered by rigid, mechanical rules, even ones wrought by myself with exotic or esoterical fixtures.

Surrounded by thousands of books, in the silence of the reading rooms, I felt my own mind multiplied by the discourse of the invisible, mostly defunct, elite. My mental processes seemed to become articulated within a single universal text, in whose interstices I involuntarily inserted my own thoughts, which seemed derisory and commonplace. I imagined myself, nonetheless, entering into resonance with the large text of the world, until I no longer knew when I was thinking myself, and when I was being thought by others. Voices and ideas would mingle into a stream of variable flow, whose dizzying eclecticism left me breathless.

Over the years, I came to imagine (was it a blasphemy?) God Himself in the form of a Library with no beginning and no end – itself a kind of infinite spherical book, with its centre everywhere and its circumference nowhere, as the mystics say, invisible but all too real, in fact hyper-real, in whose virtuality all the words of all possible tongues, all the texts ever conceived or conceivable, interwoven in an unlimited, transcendent hypertext, identical to the Logos himself, would exist. And not just all the words, but also all the signs of all possible kinds of languages would be "there," suspended in that extramundane hyperspace, vibrating like nodes, knots or vortices of meanings interconnected with all the others, in a maximum, endless intertextuality, generating and containing the things of the world like divine reasons. Later I was to find out that someone, a Byzantine monk of the seventh century – called Maximus, no less – had even given them a name: *logoi*....

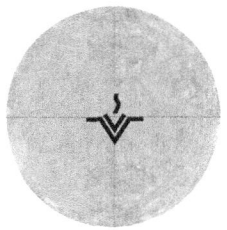

3
FANYA

But then I met Fanya. She had replaced the elegant, sad lady in the professors' room at the University Library. In 1988, the pretty redhead had finally managed to emigrate to the United States by marrying an eccentric Texan professor, who was writing a biography of Mircea Eliade, and had come to Romania for unbroached material. As for Eliade, the American didn't get much, because of the hostility of the communist authorities which put spokes in his wheels at every turn (including microphones in his room at the Intercontinental Hotel). However, maybe also as some kind of revenge against the regime, he got himself an attractive wife – though not for long, as it turned out. It was all part of a dream that she had been secretly fostering for many years. In fact I had chanced to hear about it: once, while I was taking a break, munching on a bun in the sumptuous hallway of the library, Ioana – this was the librarian's name – had told me, in a moment of depression, while she smoked her menthol Camel purchased in the diplomatic shop with illegally acquired hard currency, that she was dreaming of traveling to Brazil. Why there, of all places? She had answered most naturally, as if nothing could be more obvious – and more irresistible – than a desire to see the Amazonian rainforest, the geoglyphs, the crocodiles.... She gradually made a confidant out of me – maybe because she had no one else to tell her story to, or because something in my quixotic lifestyle of a book dweller had won her trust. Thus she came to tell me about the Texan professor who had proposed to her – a tale in which it seemed to me I had no stake. I was wrong, as we so often are about events that we believe to be of no concern to us but later prove to have been crucial, linked to people who unknowingly mark our lives.

Anyway, Fanya herself was to give me the appalling news later. She heard from another colleague in the library, who had been invited by Ioana's parents to a commemoration service, that eventually the redhead had been devoured by crocodiles in the Amazon jungle of her dreams. I remembered a quote I had once copied in my diary: *Death turns every life into destiny.* I wondered if her dream had been a premonition, or maybe the calling of an atrocious fate, and her terrible death – the price paid to some cruel gods for the fulfillment of her fantasy, or perhaps just a sacrifice offered in some other, incomprehensible order of reality, so that I might meet Fanya, her replacement. I thought of the man in John: 9 who had been born blind for the works of God to be made manifest in him, of the death of Patrocles which led to the victory of the Greeks over Troy, of the three assassins in the movie *Hero*, who sacrificed themselves so that the fourth one should be able to come face to face with the emperor Qin Shi Huang, and of a few other mysterious causal chains which escape our understanding.

*

I fell in love with Fanya naturally, immediately, and definitively. It was a cold day of March, the spring equinox. It had snowed during the night, and the city was mired with slush, smirched by exhaust fumes and dirt. I was happy to find myself in the labyrinthic, logocentric heaven of the library again. I entered the usual room and signed in the readers' registry, while incidentally noticing that the librarian, who at that moment had her back to me and was talking to a reader, was new: another silhouette, another style of dress, another coiffure, another shade of hair color – brown, cut short. Exactly then she turned towards me to take my permit, and I suddenly felt my legs sink under me and my breath taken away. She objectively seemed to me the most beautiful thing I had ever seen.

Haikus and Eminescu evoke the cherry flower; Keats – an urn; Eliot – the Ionian white and gold. These images, and a few others, came to my mind in a split second, only to be immediately repudiated as incapable of suggesting her air of calm golden mystery. It was like a recognition, an anamnesis from a past life in the realm of archetypes, a recollection of something I had known and forgotten. Now I knew, in that mysterious yet unmistakable way in which every man knows, in a certain moment of his life, that he has met his destiny. She looked me in the eyes and smiled gently – that imponderable, all-sympathetic smile which always brought to my mind the strange thought: *This must be how angels smile.* I asked her where Ioana was, in a tone of voice which I somehow managed to make sound natural, although I knew not how.

She didn't seem surprised at all, as if she had expected me to talk to her, and to ask her precisely that improbable question. She looked around with discrete implication and beckoned me with a soft, barely perceivable head bobble, to follow her, so as not to disturb the handful of tired readers, grey-haired professors who were dozing away with their heads on the tables, watched by green-shaded lamps. She opened the door to a room adjacent to the professors' hall. The sumptuous walls with marble engaged columns, gilded mirrors and gypsum plasterwork, contrasted with the grimy slush outside. Through the large windows on the upper floor, from the wing where we were standing, we could see the Crețulescu Church and the dull building of the Central Committee of the Party. It had started to drizzle over the drab city of sad, leafless trees, with wet black boughs like charred bones in a scorched wasteland, planted along mired streets where stray pedestrians were drifting with a despondent look in their eyes. But I no longer saw the rain of liquid ashes, no longer perceived the sallow bleakness of a universe with the texture of lead. I was levitating in the golden glory of her smile.

"*Here some books have ears,* she said. *Dogears, you know...*" I laughed at the double meaning of her joke. So what if we could be overheard? I didn't care. I wasn't afraid of the dreaded *Security*, the secret police which was said to have microphones everywhere. I wasn't afraid of anything. I was floating in the hot air around her frail body, on the hazel laser beams of her unworldly eyes. She had a charming voice, with a warm, evanescent ring, as if she was, and yet wasn't quite all there. She somehow made me feel like we were old acquaintances, although with no trace of ambiguity.

I told her what I had heard from Ioana about the beginning of the idyll with the Texan professor, up to that moment. Now it was no longer a secret. It had become official. She confirmed what I already suspected. She had heard that Ioana had been fired, but knew nothing more. I was not surprised to hear that retaliation had started. Usually, after a Romanian citizen

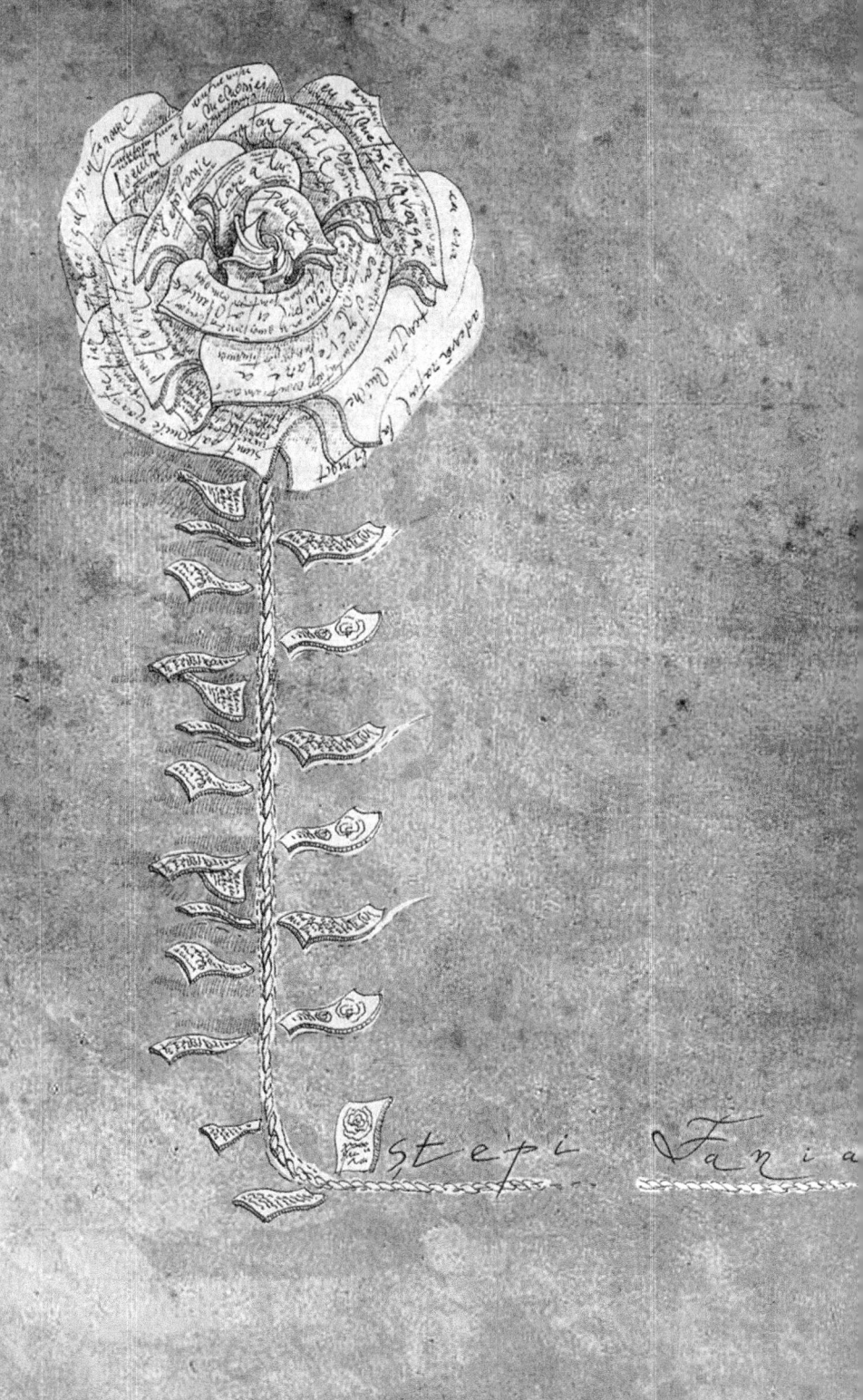

submitted to the State Council the application documents for marrying a foreigner, officially requesting a passport and permission to emigrate from Romania, all sorts of pressures and persecutions followed, including the cancellation of the labour contract under various false pretexts. The issuing of the necessary approvals could take years – or less, if the foreign citizen had high connections and could mobilize diplomatic interventions "at the top." It also depended on the country of destination – and the United States was privileged; the approval was usually given much faster when an American was involved. It seemed the Texan meant business and was effective, calling upon a group of Republican congressmen who persuaded President Reagan to intervene through the embassy directly to Ceausescu. But all that was only going to happen in the following months; for the moment all I knew was the romance with the professor of history of religions, the Eliadephobia of Romanian authorities, and Ioana's Amazonian dream. It was, however, enough to start a conversation with Fanya, from whom I made no attempt to hide the dazzling impact she had on me.

As we reentered the reading room, I had a vision of the oak boiserie on the walls burning in a weak, iridescent light, and of the books shelved along them glowing in a rainbow of immaterial flames, like a fire of the mind. Suddenly, I had an intuition that these spectral flames could be an ill omen of the future, a foreboding of their fate, presaged and foreshadowed in some inexplicable way.

Surprisingly – I could hardly understand what she could have possibly seen in me – Fanya responded with a love that no one, starting with myself, had expected. I proposed to her after three weeks, on a bright blooming Saturday in April, offering her a huge, rather conventional bunch of white roses. She accepted both the roses and the proposal on the spot, although she confessed that roses depressed her (*I am myself but the shadow of a rose,* she said, *beauty is elsewhere!*). However, she warned me again, as we had already talked about it, that she was also contemplating another path, although she wasn't sure yet. This, she said, was more in the way of an attempt, in order to see if a family was indeed her calling, or she had another vocation. I answered that I understood her perfectly and I was joyfully taking my chance. In fact, I understood nothing. For one can only understand faith by believing, and pain by suffering. But I knew it mattered no more. I felt like some gigantic, inconceivably fine crystalline mechanism had been set in motion, and that I could sooner bring the solar system to a halt than

25

the pre-established progression of this inexorable clock made of light and feelings. I was happy.

We were married in June, in the St. Sylvester church which I found out she had attended since childhood and where she had her confessor. A mixed lime-and-honeysuckle fragrance still lingered in my street, once more belying its name. I never regretted my decision. Should I add what the reader has probably already guessed? In the jungle of books pervading the house I had inherited, Fanya entered the role of Ariadne with a natural grace which seemed to indicate predestination once more.

*

Can an encounter with miracle be ignored? Once encountered, can it be ever forgotten? I had given her the name Fanya, from Stephanie, and I would sometimes jokingly call her Stepiphany, telling her that she was to me like a revelation of divinity, a tangible epiphany, her face – a manifestation of God, and other such exalted apophthegms. Every time she would invariably answer, in earnest and slightly sad, that this was blasphemy, and mildly asked me to stop. Likewise, when I called her my Beatrice, she would reply that I knew not what I was saying, but that one day I would understand basic things which I had not yet grasped, although I had read Dante: that the true labyrinth is made of our own passions, and that the Inferno and Paradise are places of the memory with reverse symmetry. And she always ended with the same sentence – *the true Ariadne is Theotokos* – which I knew not how to decode.

Although she was beautiful, she had nothing of that proud air of splendid women, that finely-arrogant expression which seemed to pity all the other, less lucky ones, and to despise all men who would never rise to the privilege of being noticed. On the contrary, her face seemed to mirror a modesty as if derived from the *Paterikon*. Her unusual charm, her eyes which seemed to be always looking toward some kind of *beyond* that was extremely familiar to her, her complete, definitive, absolute detachment from the things of this world, the soft tones of her elusive voice, her unostentatious intelligence and erudition seemingly acquired without effort, her frank, unaffected demeanor, but above all her humbleness, her delicate compassion towards her fellow human beings, and her love of God, that she tried neither to show off nor to hide, made any meeting with her not merely a memorable moment, but simply one of those events which can change one's life.

And indeed, my life was radically changed; my bookish joys gave place to a much more tangible happiness. Her love wove my existence into an entirely new text, with which I totally identified myself, for as long as it lasted. It was like a dream from which you never want to wake up: the love, the conversations, her prayers that I could never quite comprehend, the books we read together....

Happiness is not narrable, it has no history. Events can be told, happenings can be transposed onto the syntagmatic axis of temporal succession; facts can be recounted, places where they occurred can be described, in more or less detail. But the mental state in which they occurred, the emotional aura in which they basked, the unspeakable fabric of their inner experience, the only one which matters, remains largely beyond discourse. During the first two years after our marriage she continued to work at the library, and I went there as before. On clear summer evenings we walked in the streets around – Autumn Street, Harmony Street, Virtue Street, Future Street, – and when the sky, glimpsed through the foliage of chestnut trees, would become violet, we returned to the other library, which we called "home." It was as if we lived in a sphere of golden light, almost completely removed from the world around.

The morning of December 21st, 1989 found us in the professors' room, which felt under siege. We watched together, through the window, live moments in the drama of a revolution staged by professional directors. We saw the crowd gathered in the square, under the southern facade of the library, to listen to the final speech given by Ceausescu from the balcony of the Central Committee. Then followed the hooting (*We are the people, down with the dictator!*) "spontaneously" triggered at one discreet command, the panic, the scattering of the demonstrators. We left the library and mingled with those who were heading towards the University Square. I took Fanya home. Then the repression started.

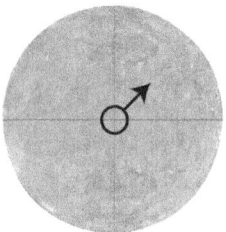

4
FAHRENHEIT '89

The next day, alone, I went downtown along with hundreds of thousands of other people. I saw the flight of the presidential couple by helicopter from the roof of the Party Central Committee building, and I joined in the euphoria of a city which lived the fall of communism like a historical catharsis. In the evening I reached the Central University Library at the same time as the tanks. Then I witnessed that infamous bibliocide, useless and sinister like all bibliocides, perpetrated for reasons remaining still unclear until today, the most absurd thing I have ever seen.

The graceful building of the library, surrounded by tanks and burning like a torch on the Eve of that blood-soaked Christmas, in the appalling noise of automatic guns, gave me then, once and for all, the tragic, spectacular, palpable proof of the fragility of libraries, of the brittleness of knowledge, of the frailty of the spirit. The strident, mechanical barking of AKMs was oxymoronically vying with some Christmas carols. For the first time after decades of atheistic communism, the chanting praising the birth of Christ was heard from loudspeakers hanging on the ex-royal Palace (turned into an art museum in the 1950's), the Crețulescu Church, and the *Generala* building, whose northern facade – the so-called Palazzo Calcani – was now also caught by the flames which were rising atop the fountains on the ground floor, lapping around the pillars with their Corinthian capitals.

Ma luai, luai...[4]

I was looking, as if hypnotized, at the grey, heavy armored cars, the locally famous TR–77 and TR–85 Romanian tanks, designed in Brasov and made in Bucharest for defense (against the Soviets? seriously?), run aground in the horrible farce of a manipulated revolution. They were advancing inexorably, under the grey walls of the Central Committee headquarters, grating on my ears as they crawled on their clumsy caterpillar treads scraping the asphalt. Their turrets, turning around in search for the invisible enemies (maybe also inexistent, some said), carried the Romanian flag. Instead of the socialist emblem, which had been freshly carved out from the middle, each flag was exhibiting a circular gaping hole, standing – as it were – for the void left at the centre of power by the fall of the communist regime: the so-called vacuum was filled so fast that we all soon realized there had been in fact no power vacuum at all. By the side of the metallic monsters were running infantry platoons, young recruits drafted from the country-side, armed with Kalashnikov machine guns, now hijacked towards a bibliomachy devoid of any glory. About twenty war machines stopped in the Palace Square and started to shoot in all directions, particularly toward the Art Museum and the University Library, no one knew at whom or why.

Velerim și Veler-Doamne...[5]

They were firing with particular frenzy at the library, seemingly ignorant of the character of the target. "That's where the terrorists are," some said, although no one had actually seen one; only some dubious corpses, which might have been anyone's, some naked, in unnatural positions, others half-charred, in sordid whereabouts, had been briefly shown on TV. The square was soon filled with stolid, careless soldiers. Or maybe they were also just scared and confused, understanding nothing of what was going on, bewildered by contradicting orders issued nobody knew by whom, since the Defence Minister was dead, having allegedly shot himself, while the supreme commander of the army, the president of the country, Secretary General of the Communist Party, Comrade Ceausescu, the genius of the Carpathians, the driver on the engine of our history (or maybe I was mixing him up with Kim Il Sung of Korea! but did it matter anymore?) had run away,

---

4 "I betook myself..." – first line of a well-known Romanian Christmas carol.

5 The chorus of another Romanian Christmas carol (approximate translation: "We go caroling, Lord").

been arrested, and was to be executed the next day, on Christmas, along with his wife, on air, live, and then boom! dead, in view of the entire nation. A nation which was only a captive audience, made of millions of frightened viewers, the same citizens who had seen his name and ubiquitous face, for years on end, on screens, paintings, newspapers, boards, panels and posters displayed everywhere, like the grotesque icon of a stammering god of socialism, a surrogate divinity of a godless religion called Marxism, or a senile pseudo-demiurge invented by some demented Gnostics to govern a failed simulacrum of atheistic utopia, and now were going to watch them being shot in some provincial garrison, like a couple of piteous animals hunted in winter, a pathetic catch chased and cornered in the frozen forest, desperate rabbits zigzagging in the frosty field or paralyzed by headlights on the road. But, however scornful was the geopolitical game, the idea of the military shooting books was abominable. The image of the incendiary projectiles fired at random into the dark by a senseless army, the luminous trails left by the tracer bullets ripping through the library windows with a sinister noise, and setting ablaze the oak wood laquearia of the old coffered ceiling in the professors' room, *our* room, were to remain forever engraved in my mind as an effigy of the ephemerality of culture.

Trei crai de la răsărit...[6]

Almost unaware of what I was doing, seeing the flames, I instinctively entered the library building, along with some firemen, in an attempt to put out the fire. I found myself climbing together with them onto the roof of the dome, holding a fire hose pouring out water from a hydrant in the wall. For a moment I contemplated the city spreading underneath in the violet light of the December evening. The walls and windows of the Royal Palace were smashed by projectiles. I knew that inside the museum were displayed old icons, now surely hit by bullets. In a flash I remembered Yenokh Hershevich Yagoda, Stalin's minister of internal affairs and NKVD director, and his hobby of shooting icons (in Solzhenitsyn's account). At least the soldiers in the square below had no clue what they were shooting at. *Forgive them, Lord, for they know not what they do...*

Seen from above, the combat vehicles in front of the library looked like broken toys scattered on the asphalt. An ambulance was edging up among them,

---

[6] "Three Magi from the East" – first line of another Christmas carol.

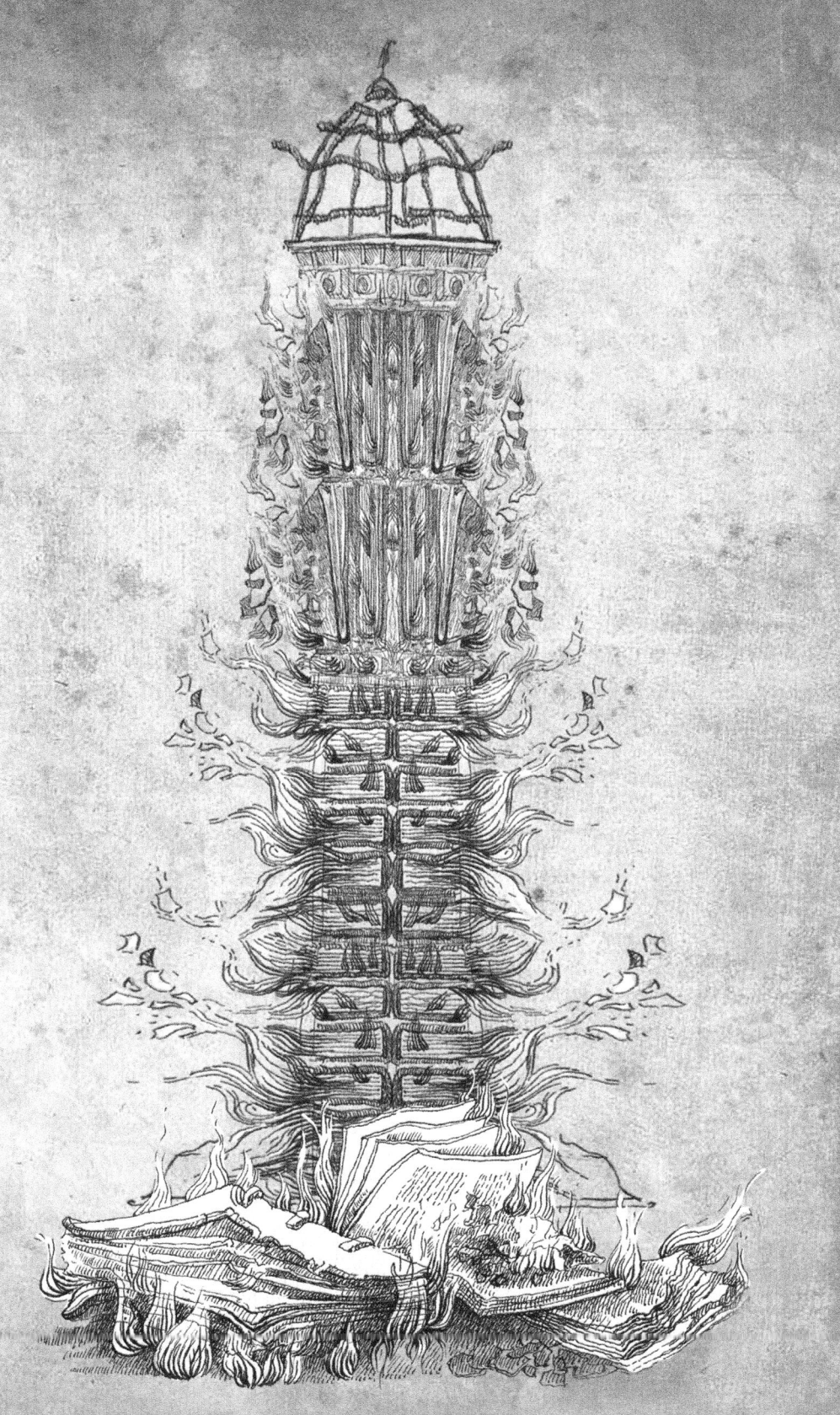

I could hear its siren as if it were right near me. The neighbouring building was still burning. It was getting dark. Suddenly the two firemen perched on the garret window and myself realized in amazement that the soldiers standing by the tanks below were shooting at us, taking us for "terrorists." We had to urgently abandon the roof. The fire was climbing towards the timber roof truss. We came down toward the reading rooms and book collections. The firemen bashed the locked doors with their axes, and we entered the professors' room. We found ourselves in a biblio-apocalypse. Amidst the flaming wainscoting, hundreds of tomes were burning on the oak shelves turned into pyres. Other hundreds of books, some of them already half burnt, were floating in the pool formed on the floor from the water gushing from the hoses. At a certain moment, while I was standing in front of a window, an AKM bullet calibre 7.69 hit me in the right arm, below the shoulder. It was just a superficial wound, a mere scratch; in fact, I felt nothing but a slight singe through the water-soaked overcoat. Only afterwards one of the firemen cautioned me about the blood coming out from my sleeve. The soldiers had fired at me, convinced they had seen, through the glass panes, against the flaming phantomatic background, the figure of a terrorist. To think that this cynically planned, erratic circus, has been called a "revolution!"

Around four a.m. a firefighting officer took me aside and told me to go home. "Anyway," the captain added, "we're also leaving."

"What about the library?" I protested.

He shrugged. "There's no point putting my men's lives at risk. Can't you see? They can get shot any time by the army. Just like you. The military have orders to shoot at everything that moves in the building."

"But, if we leave, all the books will burn. All of them!"

"So what?" The major shrugged. "Men's lives are worth more."

"But they are rare books," I insisted. "Incunabula, Eminescu's manuscripts, old hand-written Evangels, documents on the Romanians in Transylvania...!"

I couldn't believe they'd just quit. The officer lost his temper.

"So they might! My boys have families waiting for them back home. You go to their parents, wives, kids, and tell them how they died heroically, shot by the Romanian army saving some books. They'll spit in your face, knock you down... We are not to blame. Those who gave the shooting order... it's their fault, let them be held accountable...!"

And indeed, soon after that, the major gave the departure order. I had to leave with the firefighters, after casting a last glance at the inferno of scorched or burning books. The firemen's car had been pierced by army bullets. The major cursed. Standing by him, all wet and shivering, I saw how the fire was spreading, engulfing the entire building. It was going to burn for one day and one night. I wondered again, how cynical those who had ordered this horrible textual holocaust could have been? I could not help thinking it had the significance of a bad omen: the new, post-communist era was starting with an act reminding me of Bradbury's *Fahrenheit 451*. Indeed! Why could not the burning of the Central University Library go down in history as *Fahrenheit 1989*...?

But it also reminded me of something else — a historical fact, not fiction: the burning of books ordered by the Chinese Emperor Qin Shi Huang Di, the tyrant who founded the Qin Dynasty which gave its name to China. At this very moment, as they were abolishing a dictatorship, the new leaders were reiterating the logocidal gesture committed by another dictator two millennia ago in a country which was later to become communist too. In that case, should the rumors I had heard about the December "coup-olution" be confirmed, could we speak of a "Brucan-Huang-Di" bibliocide...? Could the volumes which were now burnt on the stake of a carefully planned and manipulated revolution, signify not just the end of a regime, but also a prelude, already announcing a new dystopia? It was quite likely. If yes, then it was pointing to a more subtle and perverse one than the blunt coercion which was now coming to an end.

I headed home. I passed through a place across the street from the Crețulescu Church, where later the ironic obelisk styled "The Revolution Sting" was to be erected. Exactly in that place, while I heard the rapid discharge of guns as if played back in slow motion, I had a bizarre vision. I saw how the white ashes of incinerated books lay slowly, smoothly, like a fine semiotic shroud, over the bloodied city, over the crowds which had been crying in agony, in the streets downtown, and were still shouting euphorically, *We'll die and we'll be free...!*, while they made the sign of victory with two fingers, or sang, *We won't go home, won't go away, not until we've won our freedom...* (someone had put that slogan to the macabre nineteenth-century Christy Minstrels' song, *Ten Little Niggers*! Had it been an involuntary act of cynicism, or a scoffing riddle evincing a carefully designed plan?) The millions of burnt words of the texts consumed by fire were floating over the insurgent Bucharest, falling over the population deceived once again, and ended up settling on the roofs like hot black snow made up of the imperceptible cinders of calcined letters, like a silent sign or an unheard, non-verbal prophecy...

Twelve years after *Fahrenheit '89*, on another continent, in another world, another fire was going to be staged, called by a film director *Fahrenheit 9/11*. The scenarios of subversion, manipulation and terror – so repetitive....

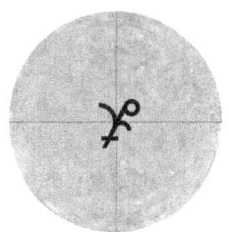

5

FLORIGERA ROSIS HALO

Soon after that, Fanya quit her library job, and in the following years we enjoyed the unexpected freedom. We travelled. Her family, already quite prosperous before 1990, and turned even wealthier after some retrocessions, helped us generously. They nurtured the same hope as I did – that Fanya should remain with us... There followed our cruises on the high seas, the voyages to our dream cities, further and further away, Venice, Ravenna, Valletta, Alexandria, Damascus, Lhasa, Kunming, Taipei... In my memory they are linked to an inexplicable feeling of heat, and a persistent taste of sea salt which would always remain in my mouth and nostrils after I touched her, or had merely been in her presence. For we were always looking for the sea, came back to it every time, watched it from the beaches of Mediterranean Africa or dived from the cliffs of Malta, the island inhabited millennia ago by Phoenician sailors speaking a Semitic language. I knew moments of perfect, absolute happiness, when the world became round and translucid like a pearl, colored in golden-purple-green like the dreams of my childhood, bitter-sweet like an almond-chocolate cake, soft and velvety like a summer twilight. Once, in the charming Maltese village 'Attard, Fanya read, on the facade of a pension overgrown with lavender, thyme, laurel, oleanders, and artemisia, a short heraldic motto in Latin – *Florigera rosis*

halo – and cried to me laughing: *Yes! Let's stay here! I wish to perfume the air with my flowers!* At that moment I realized that was the exact word: she had perfumed my life.

*

I knew, however – I had known from the very beginning, I had always been aware of it – that one day it would end, like any dream. Therefore, I was not surprised when, exactly seven years after our marriage, on a sunny Saturday in June, while we were cycling through the liquid gold of the afternoon, under the old chestnut trees lining the shore of the blue lake in Herastrau Park, Fanya told me that she would leave. She was lovelier than ever, riding a silver-colored city bicycle with her seemingly jointless legs dressed in white pants made of thin cloth. The sun reflected on her short brown hair, and her extraordinarily clear irises looked me straight in the eyes with unyielding tenderness.

We had actually talked about this many times, since the very first day, like a hypothesis or a still indistinct calling. But that which had been a mere possibility, perhaps even a probability, had now effectively become a decision. She even knew the place: she was going somewhere in Banat, a faraway region in the west of the country. The distance to Bucharest was rather one extra argument, being meant to add also a geographical remoteness between her new condition and the old existence that she was leaving behind.

Thus, I simply acknowledged, without much surprise, the news that Fanya would go and become a nun. I helped her pack a few personal belongings and drove her to the Gara de Nord railway station. She had asked me – oh, ever so gently – not to accompany her to the convent, which was located in an isolated area in Caraş-Severin, near the border, close to the Nera Canyon, which we had seen together. I suffered, no doubt, because of the separation, but the tenderness and love with which she surrounded me up to the very last moment somehow made the pain just bearable. Besides, I thought this moment, for which I had prepared myself all along, was in a way my destiny. But now I learned that which we all know: when pain arrives, preparation is of little help; its intensity is the same.

I never doubted her last words before parting: "I shall be always praying for you." What I did not anticipate were the consequences. That I could think of nothing else was to be expected. After all, she had filled, indeed she had *been*, my life for the last seven years. But something more happened;

starting on that day, something was changed in my life and my identity. On Sundays, during the Liturgy, I would try to follow every word, I read *The Philokalia* and, feverishly, the *Lives of Saints*, which I found captivating. In a way I felt as if something of her personality had been transferred to me, paradoxically, much more than when she was present. I caught myself trying to fill the void left by her absence, making her gestures, uttering her words, mimicking her intonation, thinking her thoughts, involuntarily attempting not merely to copy her, to outwardly imitate her, but to take on, to actually assume, the secret essence of her being; *to be her*.

For the next five years I lived like in a trance, without realizing very clearly what was happening to me, and why. I was no longer sure who I was, nor if my life was real anymore. I had the diffuse feeling that I had survived my own inner death, in order to live *her* posthumous, unlived life: an alternative life that she was never going to live.

Then, on the first day of a golden September, I learnt from a common acquaintance that, exactly one week later, on the feast of the birth of the Holy Virgin, Fanya would take her monastic vows. Without trying to notify her, in order not to trouble her as she had asked, I decided to go to the Nera Hermitage and witness this moment, whose significance, however, I still did not grasp.

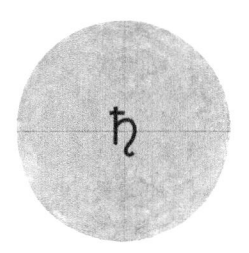

6
PHOTINI

It was for the first time that I attended a monastic tonsure rite. I knew almost nothing about the profoundly mystical ritual whereby a woman or a man dies to the world and is born in a new hypostasis, offered to Christ. I watched tensely, from a corner at the back of the tiny chapel of the nunnery, every detail of the service. And when Fanya – *my* Fanya – dressed in a long white shift touching the ground, lay down on the floor in the middle of the narthex, under the Pantocrator painted above, in the dome of the small wooden church, face down and arms stretched in the form of the cross, like a tall white rose freshly cut, I burst into tears. I cried all through the heart-rending hymn *Thy Fatherly Arms*, and I thought that, like almost everyone else, I had also wasted my life in sins.

I looked at her for the last time. It was Fanya's face, and yet it wasn't hers anymore; from now on, the face belonged to Photini – that was the new name she had been given upon taking the habit. In her new monastic garment, her head covered by a circular *kalimavkion*, she was looking straight into the flame of the candle she was holding in her hand, and which she was going to carry like that for a week. I was no longer quite sure whom I was looking at: Fanya or Photini?

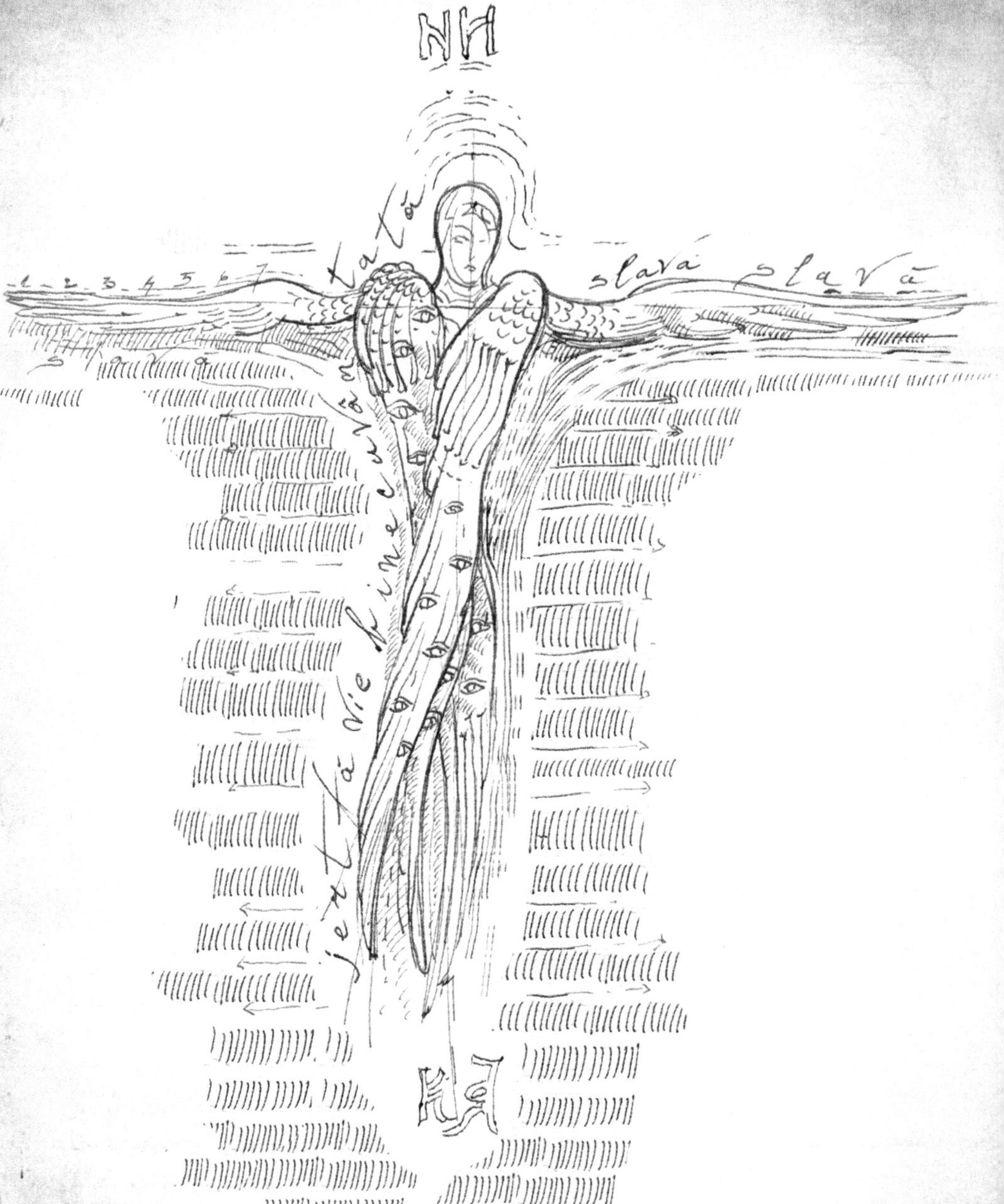
NH
1 2 3 4 5 6 7
slavă slavă

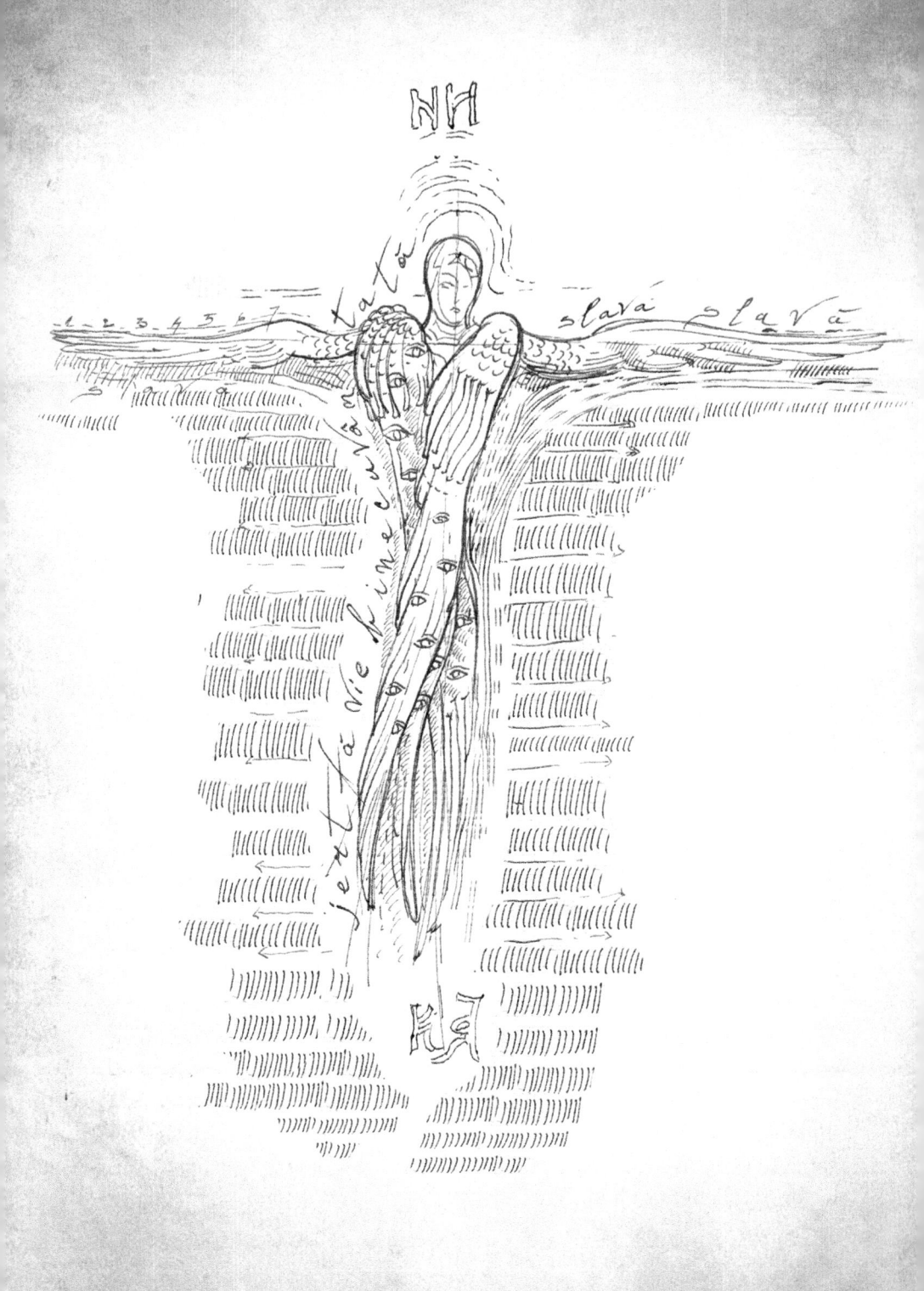

Distressed, I went out of the wooden church. I could still hear, reverberating inside, the crystalline voices of the young nuns in the choir. Their chanting was pouring out into the clear early autumn night, floating like white birds which were drawing ever wider circles over the hills around covered with birch woods. It was *Axion Estin*, to a tune composed by Anton Pann (Fanya had taught me to love psaltic music[7]): *It is truly meet to bless thee, Theotokos, ever-blessed and most pure mother of our God...* The limpid sounds were lingering above the trees, caressing the leafage, the mountain cowslips, meadowsweets, and forget-me-nots in the glades, the blueberries and cranberries sprinkled on the slopes, and disappearing – like spirals of smoke from a censer – into the fragrant air.

Disappearing? But does anything, ever, really disappear? Is anything, ever, truly lost? Verily, isn't everything, absolutely everything, preserved for all eternity? I remembered the akasha, the boundless karmic storehouse of the Upanishads, the etheric space, or receptacle-consciousness, where the entire reality, everything which has ever existed, would supposedly be preserved in the cyclical eternities of the Hindu universes. But indeed, even leaving aside Hindu esoterism, don't all our acts, all our words, all our thoughts, and generally all things, all sounds, all images, remain forever engraved in our immortal souls, and above all, recorded in the endless memory of the world, kept in God's infinite thought? Everything that has occurred once, all that has been said, imagined or felt one single time, is irreversibly, indestructibly, indelibly inscribed into the ineffable tissue of the unlimited divine memory.

But that meant Fanya's love would never be lost either: if it existed once, it will always exist; since I experienced it once, I would always have it. Once lived, nothing could take that joy away from me anymore, I could never be deprived of it; it will be with me throughout eternity. *What thou lovest well cannot be reft from thee,* I remembered. *What thou lovest well is thy true heritage.* So, it was true.

I saw a falling star blazing across the clear sky. Yes, I thought, it was indeed like some fairy-tale wedding, mystical marriage or *coniunctio*, with Fanya – the bride marrying a symbolic death. I remembered another September night, near Eminescu's statue in the Copou garden, when she had recited to me: *Always farther, ever further, slower and slower, comforting my soul unsoothed with a longing for sweet death.* "Why a longing for death?" I had asked her gently. She'd given me no answer, but I had seen her tears.

---

[7] Traditional Byzantine chant in the Eastern Orthodox Church.

These thoughts, these heart-rending memories, engraved, layer upon layer, onto the intertextual palimpsest of my memory, sybilinically reverberated between the parallel mirrors of the twin identical faces, repeated millions of times in the neurons of my cortex, did not appease me; on the contrary, after what I had experienced inside the chapel, they triggered in me an agony of lucid despair. Only now I came to feel a painful void, as if I had just lost someone very dear. And, as I was looking at the pointed spire of the church, which was carving a dark silhouette out of the continuum of the starry September sky, with the cross atop the roof neatly profiled against the disc of the full moon, I thought that, indeed, in a way Fanya had died, and Photini had been born in her place. Neither could it be said, however, that Fanya had completely disappeared. Fanya and Photini were inseparable, and yet opposed, like the terms of a mystical oxymoron. Outwardly, Fanya seemed to go on living as Photini, with her own conscience, all her memories, and even with her own body. And yet, in Photini's birth, as it were, Fanya had died. She was the same human hypostasis, the same body and the same soul, and yet another, renewed by an irreversible vow of serving God for the rest of her life in poverty, chastity, and obedience.

That night I could not sleep, in my room in the *archondariki*, just as I knew that Fanya, or rather, from now on, Photini, could not sleep in her cell either. Towards dawn, lying in a state of semi-lucid torpor, I dreamt of her (of them?) like a *Janus bifrons* with two identical faces, which were not, however, looking in opposite directions, but were somehow completely overlapping, though distinct, merged without losing their individuality, united under the same round *skoufos*.[8] In their impossible *coincidentia oppositorum* they formed a single face, thinned down to utter transparency, which was looking at me with the intensity of a silent embrace.

The next morning, I left without a farewell. We would meet in prayers, and then, more truly, in the unfading light, as she had once told me, using phrases beyond my comprehension. Now I was beginning to grasp something.

---

[8] Skoufos or skoufia: a soft-sided brimless cap given to Eastern Orthodox monastics at their novitiate or tonsure.

7
ʿAṬṬĀR

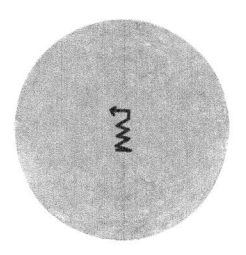

On the return trip, tired and confused, I went down to the Sasca Montana village, hailed the first car in sight without asking anything, and immediately fell asleep. The derelict Fiat happened to be going in the wrong direction, and the driver didn't care in the least where I was going. I woke up in Anina, totally off-course. Someone suggested that I take the *semmering* up to the next town, Oravita. Absent-mindedly, I got on a little toy-like train on narrow tracks, but, lost in inscrutable reveries, I barely noticed the minute, funny-looking carriages, the dozens of tunnels, bridges and viaducts over valleys with unusual, vaguely alliterative names, such as Jitin, Lishava, Carash or Shteierwald, or the spectacular, unbelievable landscapes, like from the Grimm Brothers' fairy tales.

Once I finally arrived in Timisoara, I bought a ticket on a night train to Bucharest, to the departure of which I still had a good few hours. I wandered randomly through the familiar streets of the city, crossing the Bega River on several bridges, or perhaps several times on the same bridge. In fact, I seemed to recognize the Decebal Bridge, the one where the massacre of December 17th, 1989, had been committed by the communist regime, when the victims' corpses had been taken by truck from the *Comtim* pig farm to the Bucharest crematory, incinerated, and the ashes thrown in a canal (the so-called *Operation Rose*). At some point I realized I was going in circles. In order to evade the labyrinth of streets and canals, I entered the large cathedral in the centre, where I prayed for a while, with the joy and peace given by the certainty that, at the same time, Photini was praying for me too.

At dusk, walking toward the station, soaked by the rain which had suddenly started to pour, I took shelter in a murky bookshop in the Josephin district. Once I entered the store, I felt obliged to buy some books as justification, but maybe also prompted by a need to regain, after the inner earthquake I had experienced, a long-neglected cultural identity. Besides, I was somewhat afraid to remain alone with my thoughts for eight hours on the train.

Sitting on my seat in the empty carriage, slightly shivering in my wet coat, I started to browse through the heterogenous collection I had purchased at half price: volumes 1 and 10 of *The Philokalia*, Lossky's *The Mystical Theology of the Eastern Church*, *The Eros of Divine Hymns* by St. Symeon the New Theologian ("Fanya knew them by heart" – I found myself again thinking of her as if she had died), *The Life of Saint Gregory Palamas* by Staniloae, Dante's *Divine Comedy* (just the *Paradise*, in Cosbuc's translation), and some recently reprinted stories by Borges. This last one I had bought mostly due to another kind of nostalgia, or maybe of snobbery: the translators were my former university professors, affectionately called *Doña Cristína* and *Don Andrés* by successive generations of students. *"El más cortés es Don Andrés,"* I remembered the Spanish literature classes of the accomplished *caballero*, my courteous teacher who had spoken to me for the first time of San Juan de la Cruz, in a small room on the fourth floor of the university, which seemed to float like a hot air balloon above an unreal city – like the dining room rising to the sky in a story by Scott Fitzgerald that I had read surreptitiously while serving my obligatory year in the army, during the long hours spent lying in frozen holes on the training fields under the grey winter sky, – gliding over Ceausescu's portraits, Lenin's statues, and slogans about communism (the bright future of mankind, an elusive era, the ever dimmer, hazier mirage in which no one believed any more), carried away in the obscure night by a Spanish mystic's burning poems about the steps of ecstatic love climbing toward the union with an unpronounceable Creator.

In the dim, blueish light of the railcar, I read a few Philokalic pages by St. Isaac the Syrian on the ascetic struggle and monastic life, dwelling for a while on Chapter 24 about the signs and fruits of love and mystical ecstasy.

It seemed too high for my level, but I experienced an inexplicable feeling of warmth and joy, which only lasted for a moment. I thought of Fanya.

I put *The Philokalia* aside, and started to re-read Borges' fantastic prose, which had once enthralled me, in a life I had almost forgotten. I went, as if for the first time, through the strange tales which had the gift of making me forget anything else. And when I reached the story called "The Zahir," I stopped, for no apparent reason, at the passage about some implausible *Book of Things Unknown*, or *Asrar Nama*, attributed to 'Aṭṭār. I remembered the Maltese village with a similar name, 'Aṭṭard, where she had been so happy. Could there be some Phoenician connection? Maybe not, but the link had already been formed in my mind.

I remembered the name had also intrigued me on the first reading, years ago, and I supposed, just as I had done the previous time, that it must have been the fruit of Borges' well-known pseudo-epigraphical predilection. Therefore, I took for granted the implicit assumption that it was no more than an imaginary book, a title made up by Borges himself, according to his habit of giving false quotations from inexistent authors and books never written. Nonetheless, more like an exercise meant to distract my attention, or so I thought, I tried to fancy what could be the content of a book with such an enigmatic name.

Of the multiple meanings allowed by this rather ambiguous title, given my state of turmoil, I chose an extreme one: it had to be a book about things unknown to, and unknowable by, anyone; an inconceivable text about things that nobody has ever known, or could come to know. Evidently, I picked a fantastic interpretation, somewhat metaphysically contaminated, convinced that this was the significance intended by the narrator who called himself Borges.

At this point, lulled by the repetitive sound of the wheels clicking over the narrow seams between the abutted rails, as I glimpsed through the window the Danube glittering faintly in the light of a hazy half moon, somewhere close to Orshova, I fell asleep. Inevitably, I dreamt of Fanya again. She was conjunct with Photini, clothed in her slightly too large frock. She was looking at me with unbearable kindness, through the dark veil, leaning against a rounded iconostasis colored in gold, purple, and emerald, whose icons were metamorphosing – as things do in dreams, anamorphically telescoped – into a spherical library with thousands of volumes, on whose curved golden spines the same title was infinitely repeated: *The Book of Things Unknown*. The letters were burning dimly, like a phosphorescent grass, reflected in

CARTEA LUCRURILOR NEȘTIUTE
CARTEA LUCRURILOR NEȘTIUTE
CARTEA LUCRURILOR NEȘTIUTE

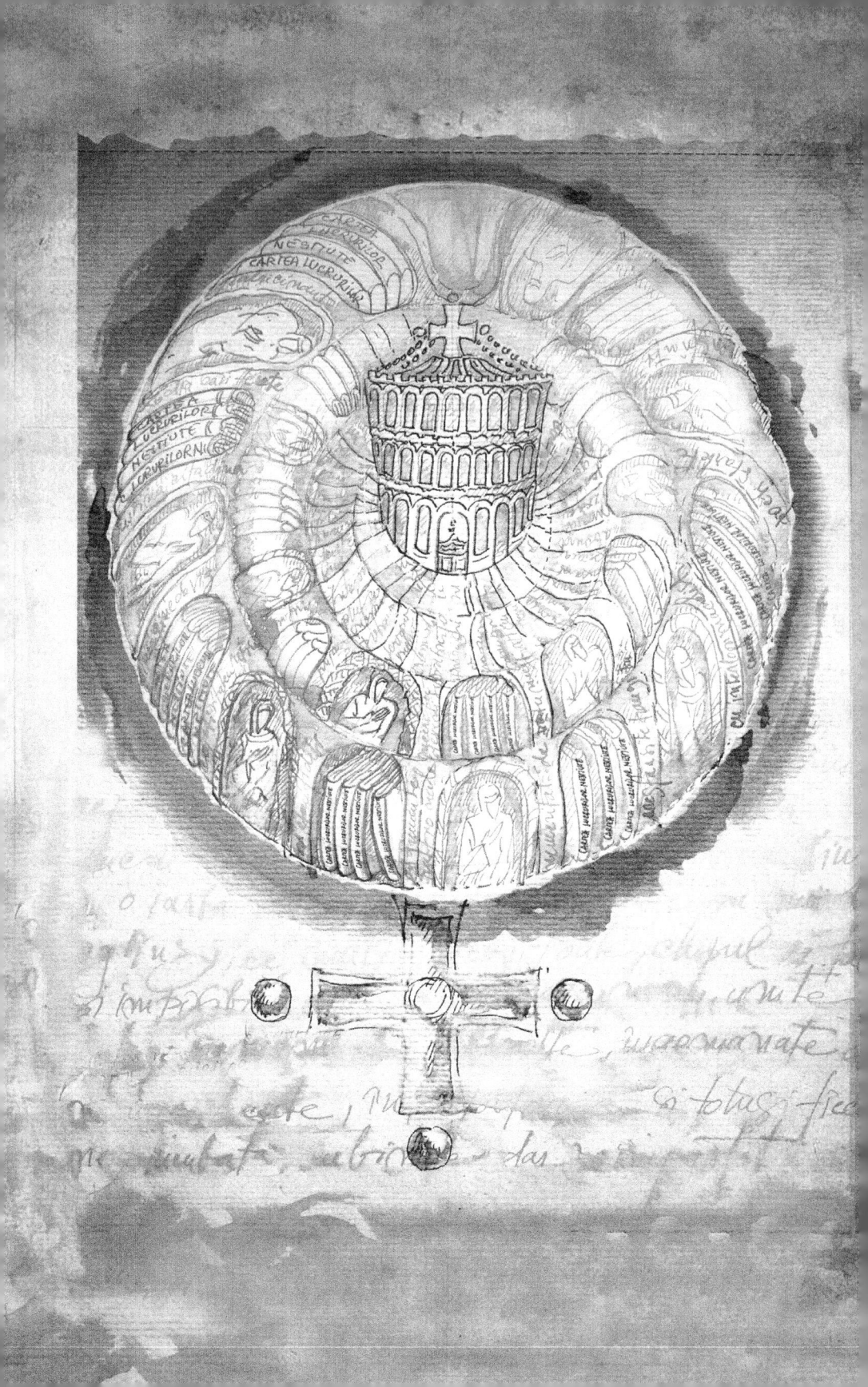

thousands of mirrors which were all multiplying her face. Fanya and the impossible book were overlapping, united and yet remaining distinct, entwined but unmerged, intermingled and yet unchanged, joined but undivided, clearly outlined and yet inseparable (something of that kind, I was to remember later, had been said about the union of the two natures in Jesus Christ undergoing no confusion, no change, no division, no separation), in a single incandescent image: a fiery palimpsest, on which an unseen hand had written another identity, without deleting the first one.

In the morning I woke up in Bucharest, frozen stiff. I got off the train, faltering, onto the platform of Gara de Nord, with the beginnings of a fever due to my extreme tiredness, the evening rain, and the draft in the cold carriage. I vaguely realized that the last image in my dream had already become a familiar thought. Fanya/Photini and the title of the book had somehow merged, or rather the title had somehow replaced Fanya in my mind. With a rest of lucidity, I tried to provide an explanation: perhaps it was better this way, the thought of my former Fanya was too painful. But then the metabolism of the station – strange intermediary body, a hybrid mutant resulting from a shopping-mall and a rusty metallic hydra, crossbred under the star sign of the railroad, an equivocal territory of transition between the captivity of urban routine and the free horizons of the world – swallowed me like a portal, and then disgorged me into the dedalus of the capital, my tragic, searing, hallucinated city, with mobster parliamentarians, non-vertebrated politicians, and other specimens of the predators' tribe, stuck in the immoral gelatin of another, endless transition with interlopers, manele singers, poets, starlets, and saints.

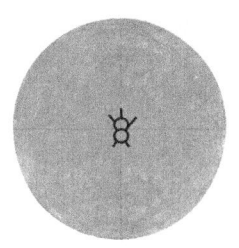

8
THE BOOK ABOUT THE QILIN

The pneumonia, in a galloping form, lasted two months, during most of which the fever kept me in an ambiguous state, bordering delirium. The dream on the train became recurrent, until I could no longer distinguish it from the confused waking state.

When at last I recovered, by mid-November, due to Fanya's parents and some faithful friends who looked after me with undeserved devotion, I found that the title of the book had turned into a real *idée fixe*. I kept trying for a while – or maybe I only pretended I was trying – to get rid of the magic exerted by the damn title. I told myself, again and again, without too much conviction, that it was a mere name invented by Borges with pseudo-erudition (although that did nothing to reduce the strangeness of the contradictory syntagm). I brought to myself various, wholly rational arguments, that it was an absurd, pointless idea. Hoping that I would forget the obsessive book, I set about writing a tale about an imaginary manuscript found in China – an older project. The composition of this fantastic narrative took me another two months, and absorbed me enough to make me believe that I had freed myself from the inexplicable phantasm.

The story is about a text calligraphed on bamboo plates, in the fifth century B.C., by one of Confucius' disciples. The manuscript is called *The Book About the Qilin*. The disciple is Zuo Qiuming, the one usually associated with drafting the famous classic called *Chun Qiu (The Spring and Autumn Annals)* and the commentary bearing his name, the *Zuo Zhuan*. We are assured by Zuo – who is also the narrator of this first chapter of the story – that the text is not apocryphal. In it, Zuo records Master Kong's last speech, in which the sage describes and comments – with far more details than appear at the end of the chronicle itself – the famous episode of the killing of the unicorn, called *qilin* in Chinese. As if in anticipation of future speculations by Christian missionaries, Confucius speaks about the unicorn as the symbol of a Saint who will come to save mankind. The allusion is understood to refer to the Incarnation, the *qilin* being a prefiguration of Christ. Confucius dies, and Zuo is arrested when he tries to publish the master's last words. His contemporaries accuse Zuo that, under his teacher's name, he tries to circulate a fake with heterodox ideas. He is sentenced to the Death by a Thousand Cuts. Before being seized and ruthlessly executed, Zuo manages to hide the bamboo scroll.

Zuo's descendants keep it as a precious relic. One of them, Zuo Guang, saves it at the price of his life, two centuries later, during the burning of the books ordered by Emperor Qin-Shi-Huang-Di. Guang's son – the narrator of Chapter 2 – engraves the text of *The Book About the Qilin* on a stone stele, which he buries.

Two hundred and eighty-eight years later, in 67 A.D., the Holy Apostle Thomas arrives from India on a ship, landing in China's greatest harbor of the time, Lianyungang. During his preaching, the stele engraved by Guang's son is brought to light, and Thomas confirms that its prophecy has come true. Thomas' sermon of confirmation is engraved on another stele. During the persecution following Thomas' departure from China, both steles are hidden in a cave in the Lianyungang cliffs, by a Chinese convert – Xu, the narrator of Chapter 3.

The two steles are found there, nineteen centuries later, in 2025, by a French archaeologist who retraces the whole story. His death in suspicious conditions prevents its publication. This mission is assumed by his daughter, Nicole Perrier, together with her Romanian husband, Toma, a specialist in Artificial Intelligence, who is also the narrator of Chapter 4.

The final chapter takes place in 2035, in a dystopic China, where millions of Chinese converts to Christianity, including Eastern Orthodoxy, are persecuted by a pseudo-theocratic government – a sophisticated, technological-ideological-magical totalitarian regime. Toma and Nicole, turned missionaries, are martyred together with one thousand Chinese Christians, including the doctor An Mingbai. The head of the persecutors is the governor of Beijing, An's brother, the narrator of this chapter. Amazing miracles take place upon their martyrdom; hundreds of thousands of Chinese are converted, led by the former governor, now become president of China. Near the Beijing Temple of Heaven, a church is raised, called Saint Sophia of China, with the Apostles Thomas and Andrew as patron saints.

*

This intricate and implausible story was published in January 2004, and met with a certain success, due to the exotic subject matter and a style which seemed to be the fruit of hallucination. It was no accident, for my state, during the entire duration of stitching up this laborious plot, was a flutter bordering on raving. But, although I seemed to have managed to forget the other book, somewhere in the background it had always been present in my mind. I understood that in fact *The Book about the Qilin* had only been a temporary substitute for the other, much more elusive piece. It had only been a short interlude. It turned out it had been useless.

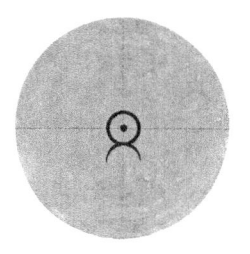

9
ZAHIR

Eventually I gave up trying to oppose the peculiar spell. Unwittingly, or maybe on purpose, I allowed myself to be haunted by *The Book of Things Unknown,* exactly as, in Borges' story, the character becomes haunted everywhere by the Zahir.

Resigned, but not without a secret self-indulgence, I did a little research. I immediately discovered that neither the author nor the title was mere fiction, as I had ignorantly assumed on a superficial reading. Farid al-Din of Nishapur, also called 'Aṭṭār, i.e. "The Perfumer," because he used to make and sell perfumes before discovering his mystical calling, had been a Sufi poet, famous in the Islamic world. Born in 1142 in Khorasan, in Eastern Persia, 'Aṭṭār was beheaded by Genghis Khan's Mongolian invaders in the horrid massacre of 1221.

One of his works was indeed called *Asrār Nāmah*, a title diversely translated as *The Book of Secrets*, of *Unknown* or *Mysterious Things*. Its text seemed to have been lost, until it was eventually discovered in Istanbul, in two manuscripts – one (F446) in the university library, the other (*Ayasofya* 4792) in the basement of the famous cathedral of that name. Like other writings from the Late Islamic Middle Ages, including some by 'Aṭṭār himself, this one also contained Sufi ideas or parables about the blindness of the soul lost in the labyrinth of the material world, and about man's mystical union with God. So the book had really been written, and it was a collection of about twenty symbolical and allegorical narrative poems called *maqālāt*. Two of them were commented on by Hellmut Ritter in *Das Meer der Seele*, published in Leiden in 1955 – six years after Borges had published "The Zahir." Anyway, nothing even remotely resembled the abracadabrish meaning contrived by me during a feverish night.

On the other hand, the so-called monograph *Urkunden zur Geschichte der Zahirsage*, by Julius Barlach, allegedly published in Breslau in 1899, was a fictitious work by an author invented by Borges.

However, the Persian encyclopedia called *The Temple of Fire* was real. A collection of biographies of Persian poets in Iran, Turan and India – a poetic history of the world's most poetic people – had truly been written around 1779. Its author, Hajji Lutf Ali Beg of Isphahan, a descendent from the Begdadi Shamlu tribe originating in Damascus, derived his name (*Lutf Ali*, "Ali's Grace") from Ali himself, Prophet Muhammad's cousin. Lutf Ali also chose for himself a poetic name (*takhallus*): Azir, Azur, or Azar (according to Islamic legends, Patriarch Abraham's father was named Azar). The book's title, *Atesh Kedah* (or *Atish Gadah*), *Temple of Fire or Temple of the Magi*, evokes fire as a metaphor of divine love. The temple of fire is the heart; in this fire of love, the roses of poetry turn into *aṭṭar*, the delightful fragrance of grace. Fire can be destructive or harmless: it can ravage and torment, like the flames of hell where the rebel king Nimrod is burning; but it can also guide or comfort, like the immaterial fire in which the bush seen by Moses on Mount Horeb burned unconsumed.

As for the Zahir, it was defined by Borges as designating, in the Muslim world, "beings or things which have the terrible power of being unforgettable, and whose images eventually drive people mad." The Zahir – Borges said – is "the ruin of all who saw it once, even from a great distance, for they cannot think of anything else till the end of their lives."

Philip Meadows Taylor's *Confessions of a Thug* was also a real book, truly published in Oxford in 1839. In his turn – Borges claimed – Taylor had quoted the words of the Muslim sage Muhammad al-Yemeni: "There is no thing or creature in the world that does not tend to become a Zaheer; but the All-Merciful does not allow two things to be a Zaheer at the same time. There is always a Zaheer, although its forms are always different."

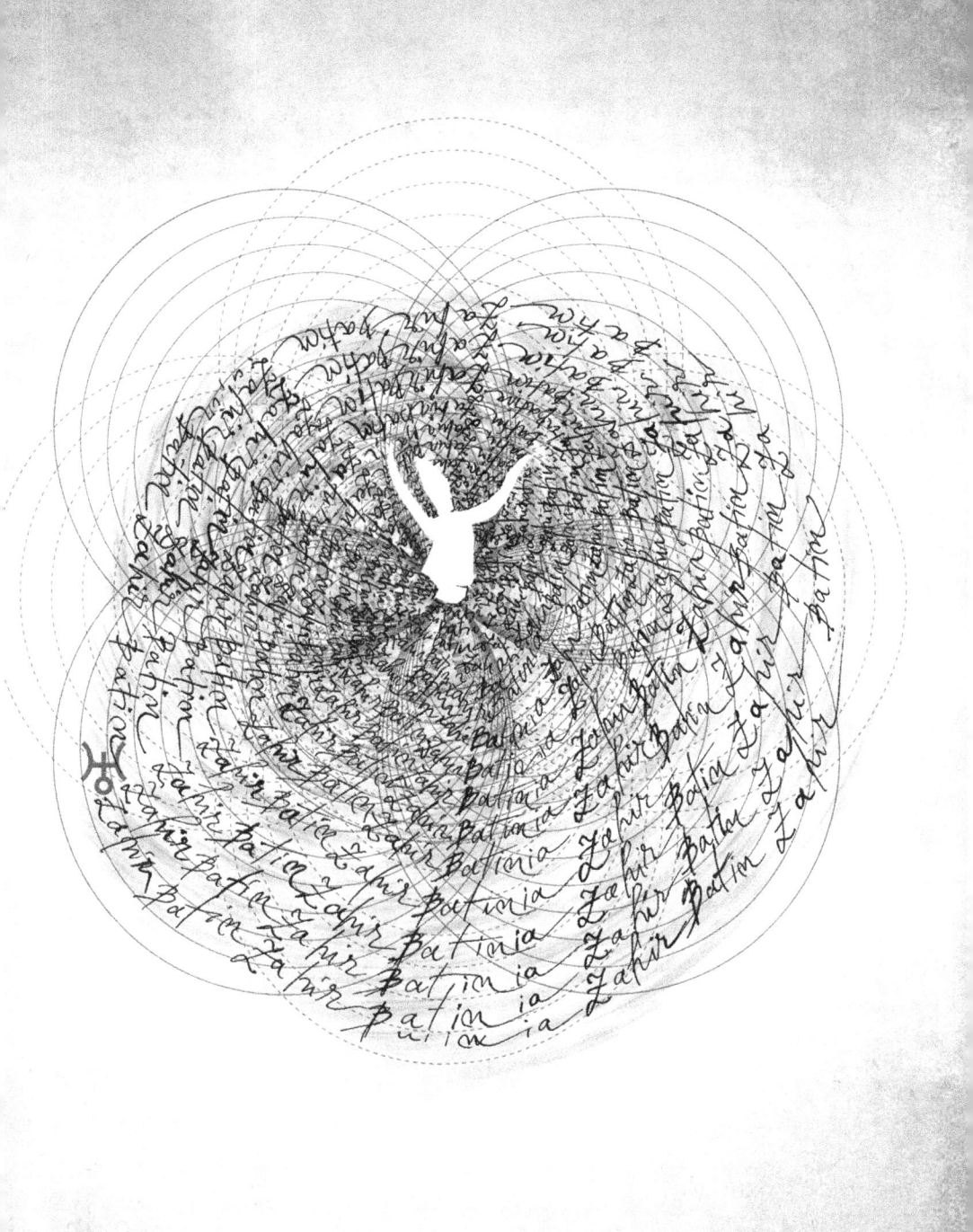
Zahir Batin

The Book of Things Unknown

In Arabic, says Borges, *Zahir* means *visible* or *evident*, being in that sense "one of the ninety-nine names of God." From various other sources I also learned that, in Islam, *Zahir* refers to the literal meaning of the Koran as a manifestation of Allah, and that *Zahiri* is an exoterical school of the verbal, cataphatic interpretation of that strange book dictated to the prophet by a spirit calling himself Gabriel. Likewise, I learned that there is also an esoterical school called *Batiniyya*, focused on the hidden, nonverbal, unutterable, apophatic interpretation of the Quran, and that the two terms, *Zahir* and *Batin*, are in fact inseparable, being the obverse and the reverse of the same reality, as two complementary ways to God, Who is above creation, but manifested in it.

Finally, I discovered that, also in the Sufi tradition, the repetition of the divine name abolishes all language and leads to the mystical experience of illumination. Of course, I thought of Eastern Orthodox hesychasm and, in passing, I wondered whether the medieval Sufi mystics might have borrowed the concept from Byzantine Orthodox monks in Egypt, Syria, or Palestine, after the Muslims had conquered these provinces of the great declining Christian empire. However, I found nothing to support this tempting hypothesis, and anyway all that was to no avail. On the contrary, instead of being lessened, my fascination turned into a compulsive pursuit.

I had to admit the self-evident truth that, just like Borges' infinite Argentinian twenty-centavos coin, the strange title, once seen, had somehow become for me a Zahir. Its three main words merged within a single, circular locution with no beginning and no end.[9] Just as the round piece of metal, in the Borgesian story, had replaced Teodelina Villar, who was herself a sign of impossible love, or rather, of some ineffable manifestation of transcendence, the contradictory triverbal syntagm replaced Fanya, becoming for me an emblem and a *trigger* of dream, of desire, and of some improbable revelation. I could no longer think of anything else, and I knew it would continue to occupy my thoughts till the end of my life.

---

[9] The five-word English title *(The Book of Things Unknown)* has only three words in the original Romanian version *(Cartea Lucrurillor Tainice)*, suggesting Simon's real obsession is the Trinity.

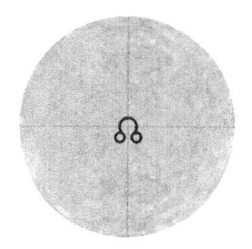

10
THE BOOK OF THINGS UNKNOWN

Predictably, from this obsession it didn't take long until I started to entertain, fearfully at first, then with hope, and eventually with resignation and fanaticism, a wild idea: if Borges had postulated the existence of this indescribable book, from which he had even quoted a tantalizing "interpolated" line (*The Zahir is the shadow of the Rose and the rending of the Veil*), and 'Aṭṭār had produced a partial (or, to my mind, imperfect) version, why couldn't I, Simon Palamas, be the one to write it myself? Or rather, better said, to rewrite it, in the "true" purport of the title, which I thought I was the only one to have glimpsed.

As to the fact that the radical interpretation I had given to that perplexing title was also implying a logical consequence which seemed to make my goal an unmistakable utopia – that, in order to be truly unknown, the objects described or the facts narrated in the book would have to be (and to remain) unknown even to myself, as an author – that was precisely what seemed to me the greatest challenge ever confronted by a writer.

It is easy to write about inexistent things: it is enough to invent them. From that moment on, they exist – their shapes are materialized in your fancy, as Shakespeare puts it: *imagination bodies forth the forms of things unknown*. But how to write about things you do not know at *all*, about which you have

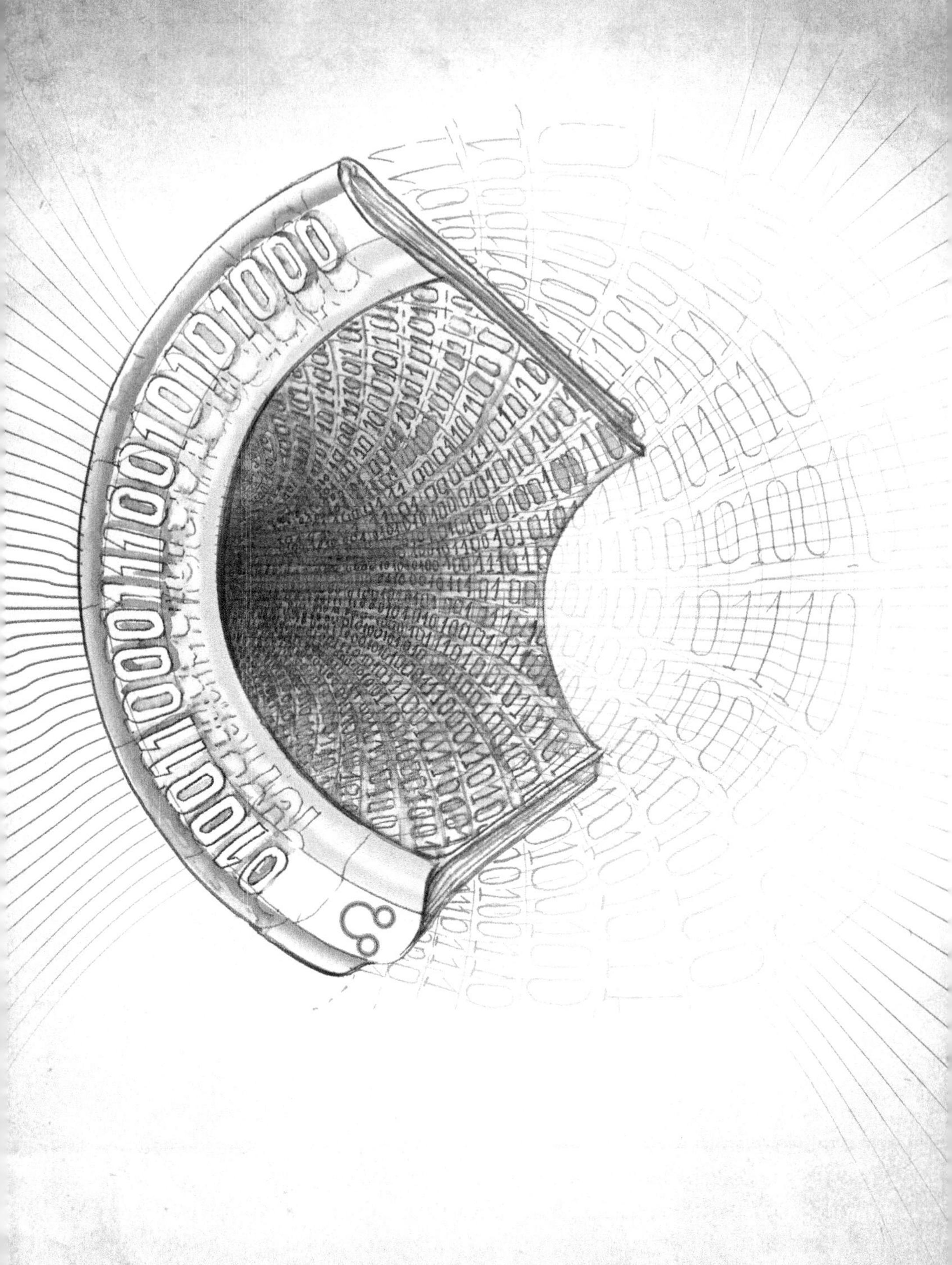

absolutely no information, not even the slightest idea? Moreover, things that you must continue to ignore even as you write about them. How to draw the atlas of an invisible territory, the map of an entirely unknown world?

The very title was an oxymoron, for the notion of a *book*, and that of the *unknown*, are mutually excluding each other: by definition, a book is an utterance, and that which is uttered – to the extent that it can be embodied in a discourse – is known. The moment you've committed to paper (I was old-fashioned, calligraphy gave me a feeling of organic, intimate contiguity with the text laid down like a trail of neurons discharged onto the white sheet of cellulose) one single word, or even a single letter about something, they would already represent minimum determinations of that thing, making it, at best, an *almost* unknown, hardly glimpsed or intuited one, but it would deprive it of the quality of a truly unknown thing. In fact, exactly the same phenomenon would occur even the very instant of a mere formulation of a thought. It was a perfect aporia.

Paul Valéry says that the real in a pure form could make the heart stop. But then, would not the unknowable, in a pure state, have the same effect? Would I not also succumb on the spot, before managing to transcribe (but through which medium, and in what language?) a single quantum of that which was revealed to me? Or, even worse, would not the impact of pure incognoscibility on a conscience – supposing it were, phenomenologically, possible – make the universe itself stop suddenly, petrified in a perfect frozen clarity, like in an instantaneous thermic death?

But I discarded that too, as mere speculation. Anyway, it did not matter anymore. I could no longer quit. It was more than a challenge. It had become the very sense of my existence. From then on, I spent my years in a feverish search for the solution, the answer to the haunting question: what could such an unimaginable book look like?

11

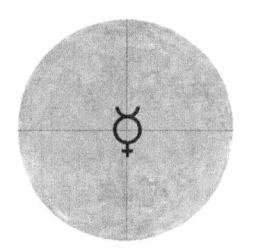

THE BOOK OF THINGS UNINTELLIGIBLE

I underwent the entire process of a definitive, involuntary and useless ascesis (if that were a fit word for a condition in which I was forgetting to eat and lost my sleep). Over the years, my body, only rarely fed with salads furnished by the same merciful friends, became frightfully thin, like a skeleton, sporting a green-bluish shade like that of Milarepa, who had been nicknamed the *Caterpillar*.

From the start I dismissed the simplistic idea of writing (another) book about God. I thought enough theology had been written already, including the apophatic branch, and anyway, we already know about God that which He has considered useful to reveal to us. Although not yet initiated into the subtleties of Christian dogma, now I knew that the Biblical revelation and Holy Tradition would contain the essentials.

*

I also rejected the idea of writing (another) *Book of Secret Things*. Long before meeting Fanya, I had known the fascination of esotericism (surrounded by thousands of books, probably I would not have been able to evade it even if I tried). For several years I had (*Habe nun, ach! Philosophie*) studied astrology and drawn astrograms on hand-copied blank charts. It took me hours to calculate, using the NASA planetary ephemerides, the positions of planets, the Zenith and the Ascendant, to map with (relative, for that matter) dexterity the celestial houses, and to trace with colored lines the planetary aspects. I had even acquired a little reputation among friends for the personalised interpretations, transits and forecasts that I made with a certain (also questionable) accuracy.

But I had not stopped there. I had grown somewhat familiar with the Tarot Arcana and the Kabbalah, the *philosophia perennis*, the occult sciences, alchemy, magic, theosophy... I had read a helter-skelter of everything I could find at home and in the library catalogues – Agrippa, Papus, Alice Bailey, Eliphas Levi, *Corpus Hermeticum*, Oswald Wirth, Dane Rudhyar, and many others better left unmentioned. I had progressed in these studies for a while, until I found myself on the brink of disaster, and, filled with dismay, depression and confusion, I had thrown away all my occult books and swore never to touch those cursed writings again.

I hadn't the slightest intention to break this promise now. Besides, it would also have been incorrect: "secret" is not tantamount to "unknown." No matter how small were the circle of those initiated into the mysteries of an esoteric teaching, they are nevertheless *known* – even if only to a tiny minority.

*

Later, while browsing through the *Book of Metamorphoses* (the title given by the translator of one version of the *Yi Jing* or *Classic of Changes*) and Joyce's *Finnegans Wake* – two of the most cryptic books I knew – I thought of producing a text so sibylline, so recondite or hermetic as to be incomprehensible to anyone, obviously including myself.

But neither did this solution seem acceptable – firstly because, upon reconsideration, I wasn't quite sure I would be capable of such an abstruse accomplishment. Secondly, because there were enough precedents: there were, for instance, the *Liber Radiorum* and the thirty-six mysterious encoded squares in the formidable astrological and magical treaty *Aldaraia sive Soyga vocor*, or *The Book which kills*, with its *literis transvectis* (*Soyga* being *Agyos* in reverse, that is the opposite of a saint, or a devil), incantations, demonologies and genealogies of angels, evoking John Dee's lythomantic, hydromantic, oneiromantic, crystalomantic and catoptromantic obsessions. Then the

Voynich manuscript existed, with its bizarre paradisiacal flora, seemingly imitating the Edenic inflorescences in Byzantine iconology, and its strange, still undeciphered writing. There was also the alchemical Ripley manuscript, containing instructions for obtaining the philosopher's stone and the elixir of eternal life, with its enigmatic homunculi and cryptic figures of dragons biting their own tails, green and red lions, human-faced celestial bodies, blooded athanors, lilies, scrolls, comets and golden birds (*spiritus volans*), beads of fire and petrified drops of blood, burning blades, stabbed books, spheres crowned by golden roses and hermetic basilisks. Another such sibylline text was the Egyptian-Etruscan *Liber Linteus*, with names of gods, sacred places of worship and rituals whereby the haruspices attempted to discern the inscrutable divine will. Although dubious, there was also the Rohonc Codex, be it an initiatory cipher or artificial language, a farce, mystification or sophisticated game, an encoded apocryph, Scythian paleoscript, or a logographic-transliterated Gospel book, a Sumerian-Hungarian, Latin- or Thraco-maniac protochronistic delirium.... Let alone the asemic exaltation of chaos and obscurity called *Codex Seraphinianus*, a surrealistic encyclopedia of an arcane imaginary world, with its encoded alphabet, organic machines and beings of composite regna with bizarre organisms. Or the *Cicada 3301* cyberenigmas – digital riddles made for internet soothsayers, with their occult, cryptographic and kabbalistic allusions. Therefore, supposing I were capable of pulling it off, what would be the point of producing one more? Finally, because it would have been once again incorrect: *unknown* to anyone is not the same as obscure or *unintelligible*.

12

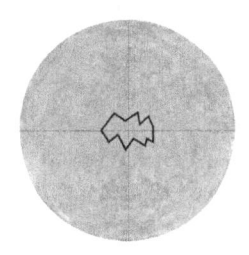

THE BOOK OF THINGS INVISIBLE

At yet another stage of my pursuits, while staring at the stack of unwritten sheets of paper on my working table, I was tempted by another thought: there, in front of me, was the book I dreamt about, already written. Maybe even a whole unseen, hidden library, a *bibliotheca abscondita*. I let myself be seduced for a while by this idea, finding arguments for it: a book about incognizable things could only be written with invisible characters, in an inexistent language. Therefore, it would have to look exactly like that: a certain number of blank pages (it only remained to be seen how many: perhaps ten thousand, which means countless for the Chinese; or one thousand and one, like Scheherazade's unending nights; or sixty-four, like the hexagrams of the infinite, circular *Yi Jing*; or twenty-two like the Tarot Arcana, twelve like the Apostles, ten like the Sephirots, seven like the days of Creation, five like the Chinese elements, four like the mystical animals of the Apocalypse, three like the persons of the Trinity, two like the natures of Christ, or even a monadic one would be enough), immaculately white, expressing perfectly pure apophatism. And if I had lost the memory of having written this invisible book, it stood to reason why: I must have written it in a dream.

For, to say the truth, I had to admit the strange fact that I was beginning to feel, like ʿAṭṭār himself (with whom I seemed more and more to identify),

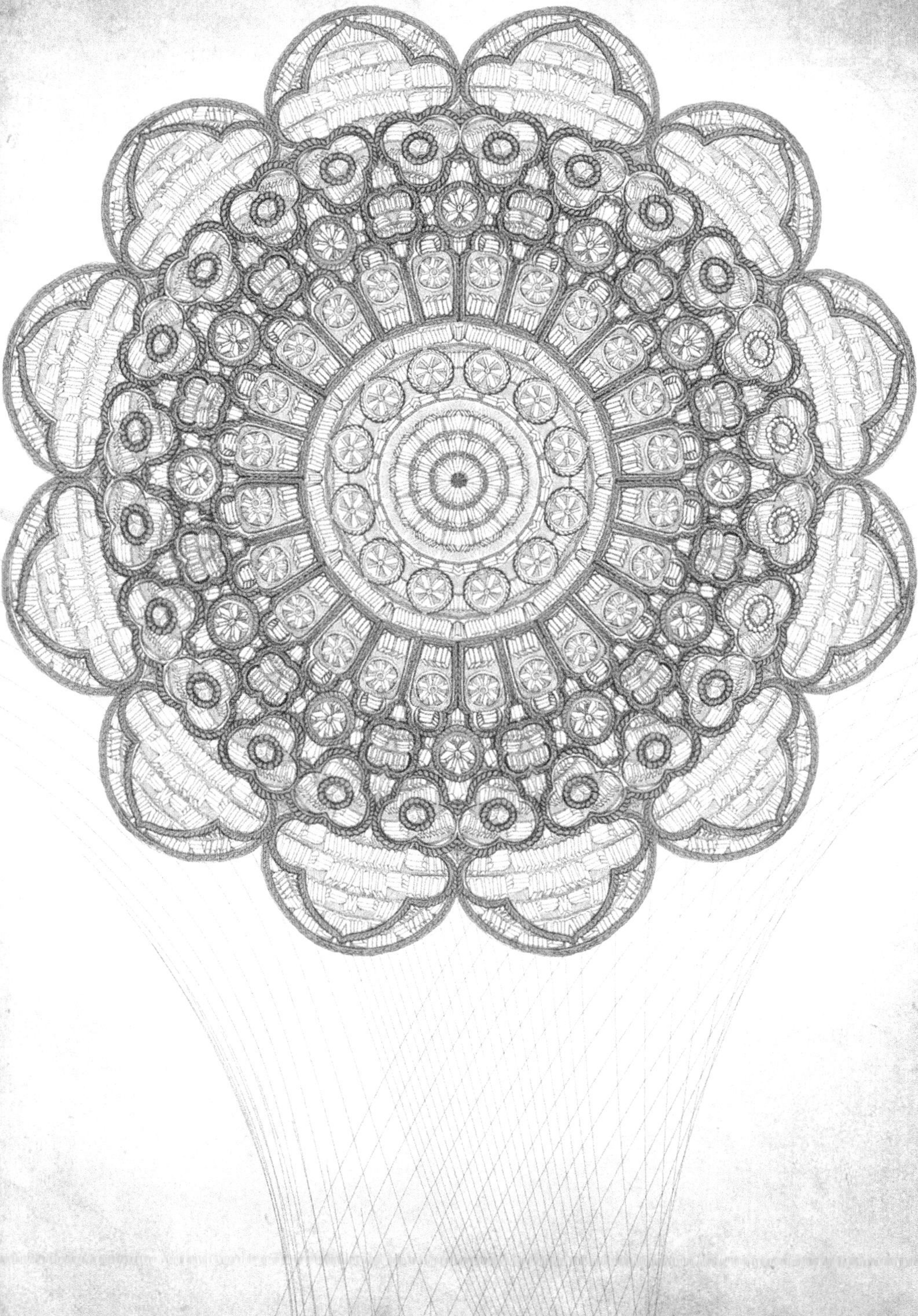

that my longing was not so much for something in the nature of writing – even a poetical one, or embodied in a book other than any other ever written – as of a mystical order. Besides, there was one more argument in favor of blank pages. If each and every word of a book incurs the risk of becoming an idol that its author may come to worship, more or less consciously, instead of the One true God, thus turning him away from the only object of legitimate adoration (it was a recurring motif in the work of 'Aṭṭār himself, which I had found, not without bewilderment, in Ritter's monograph), then a wordless book would have certainly guarded me from such a subtle form of idolatry.

But I eventually rejected that solution too, for being all too easy. I didn't want to steal my own hat. To me it had become a matter of life and death.

Moreover, there were enough precedents of this kind as well. I remembered the book with blank pages "written" for the edification of the skeptical members of the French academy by Micromegas, Voltaire's character from Sirius, and another, just as immaculate, in the farce made to Professor Openshaw in Chesterton's story, "The Blast of the Book." But there were others. One day it even amused me (if this could be said about the state of quiet, serene despondency in which I dwelled) to realize there already existed in world literature many such more or less radical "books" containing blank pages with inexistent, imperceptible or unperceivable text. There were Father Sterne's white (and black) pages, the *Final Poem* in Gnedov's *Death of Art*, De Vries' *Superabundant White*, Nichol's *Condensed History of Nothing*, Kostelanetz' *Tabula Rasa* (1000 pages) and *Inexistences* (666 pages), Lydiat's *Lost for Words*, Theonomius' *Negative Theology: An Introduction*, Cégeste's *Nudisme* in Cocteau's *Orphée*, Apicella's *Memories of an Amnesiac*, Stilinović's *Subtracting Zeroes*, Aram Saroyan's ream of paper, Idries Shah's *Book of the Book*, the anonymous *Survival Procedures Manual in Case of Nuclear Attack*, Don Paterson's poem on traveling to the Kyushu mountains to meet a Zen master whom he couldn't find, and other extravagant attempts to express the inexpressible, to lay out the absolute, the apocalyptic, or at least the void. I found them ingenious but futile, poor flippant gags or trouvailles, like Cage's inaudible *4'33"*.

13

THE BOOK OF THINGS IGNORED

The most difficult proved to be the rejection of yet another idea, a lot more tempting, because a lot more subtle.

Back in the old days, before the "Fanya era," I had yielded to the Oriental fad, like many of the (more or less) dissident peers in my generation. I had flirted with Hinduism, Buddhism and Daoism and even dreamt of travelling to China and Tibet. Later I actually went there, on a long journey to Asia with Fanya, and abandoned the idealism of *Sūnyāta-vāda*, the School of Voidness doctrine. But now I found I hadn't quite forgotten it.

I reread David-Neel's version of *The Book of Transcendent Knowledge*, the *Prājña pāramitā*, supposedly uttered by Gautama Buddha himself, and then – so the legend said – kept for centuries at the bottom of the sea by snakes, and brought later by the same said reptiles to the no less legendary astrologer and magician Nāgārjuna.

And then it hit me. It was summer, I was lying on the Black Sea shore – where the same unremitting friends had brought me, in the hope I might recover from what seemed to everyone a serious, albeit harmless, mental alienation – and I was looking at the blinding July sun, reflected in the myriad soft emeralds of the shimmering waves. And suddenly, although somewhat offhandedly at first, I was tempted to accept the notion that everything was just an appearance, a projection of my own mind, a phantasm or an infinite thought, as stubborn as it was devoid of any real existence, of my unenlightened self. I allowed myself to be carried away by the idea that the few little clouds in the sky, the great sea of jade, the shrieking gulls, the hot nacreous sand, the greenish, water-polished pebbles, the shells with fine, fan-patterned ridges and concave inlays of opaline silk, the limp jelly fish stranded like tiny gelatinous spaceships driven by weird, pellucid extraterrestrial beings which had been killed by bacteria like in Wells' novel, the thick layer of algae cast on the beach by the waves, the usual assortment of tourists sunbathing on deck chairs and kids running across blankets, screaming and splashing everywhere, and the entire scenery around me, were nothing but *maya*, a chimerical veil, a deceitful texture warped of illusions, a text with no beginning and no end, an immaterial fabric woven by my own ignorance.

If that indeed were true, it would all have been very simple. *The Book of Things Unknown* would be the world itself, seen as an infinite *Book of Things Ignored*; an insubstantial product of my own mind blinded by *avidya*, recreated each and every instant by my own ignorant mental activity. The *things unknown* would be the very things of this world, mental fabrications devoid of any intrinsic reality, illusory forms generated by my own *karma*. And this very law of causality would be the one holding me enslaved to illusion and to the oneiric projection called *samsāra*.

According to Buddhism, this whole material universe was nothing but a fiction maintained by desire, by attachment and, ultimately, by ignorance. People were only the victims of their own nescience, perpetually wandering along this relentless chain of reincarnations, in an absurd string of births, deaths, and rebirths – a never-ending cyclical return or round dance of transmigrations, known as the "wheel of *samsāra*." Nothing else but a phantasmagoric game of vain shadows – claims the Tibetan Buddhism of the Diamond Vehicle, as well as the Zen school – projected by our own mind onto the unbounded screen of pure void.

The *Prājñapāramita* claims that form is vacuity, and vacuity is form. The world itself – the *Book of Transcendent Knowledge* affirms – would have vacuity as its substrate and its essence, as an unconceivable state of the total absence of manifestation. The world is said to arise incessantly, now and at every moment, from our own mind. Being a subjective image, the world would have no other origin except mental activity, without which there would be no being, no universe.

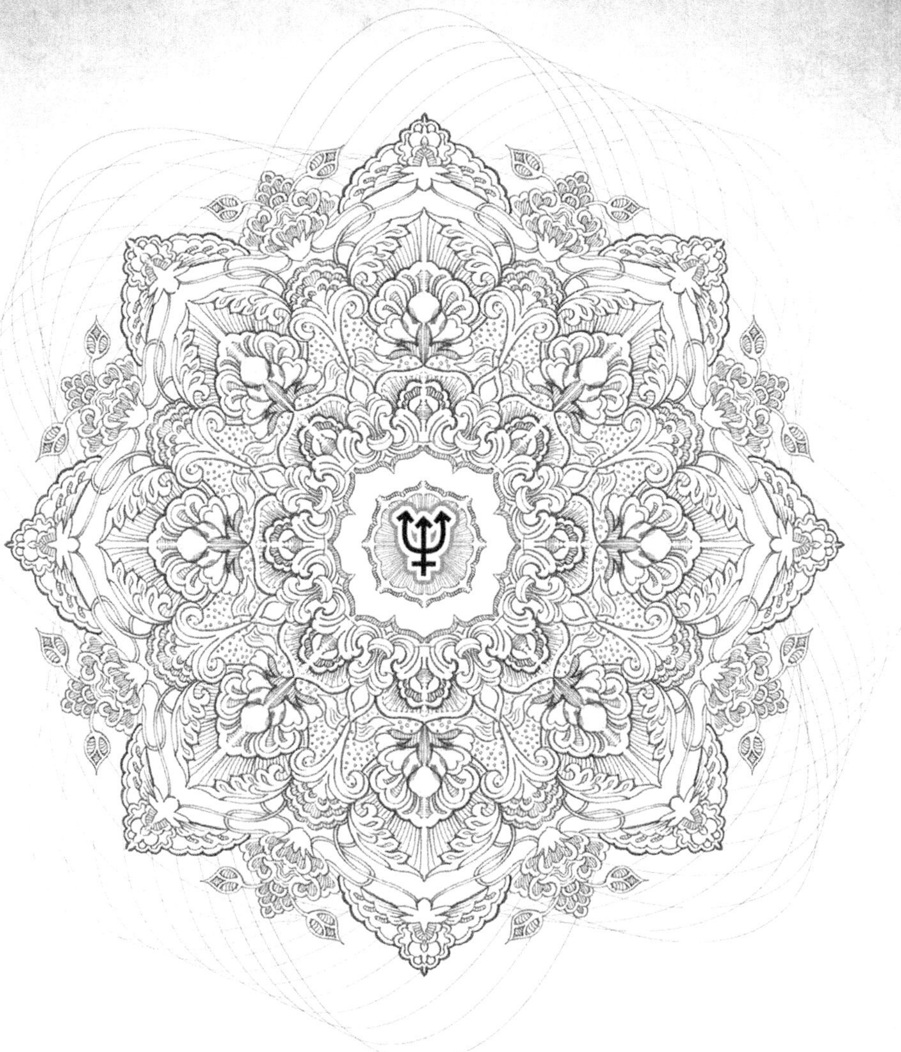

Caught in the game of this intellectual seduction, I remembered the teaching of the *Mādhyamika* School about the "Jewel of the Buddhist Doctrine": the universe itself, and each being or thing within it, would be no more, nor less, than the infinite chain of the *Interdependent*, or *Co-dependent*, *Origins* – an eternal succession of ephemeral conglomerates, endlessly decomposing into the multitude of causes which have generated them, coming from the unfathomable far recesses of eternity.

*

But I eventually also rejected that temptation, far more enticing than the others due to the sophisticated nature of the Doctrine of Vacuity. I could not accept a solution, however elegant, based on an idea I did not believe in; it would have meant lying to others, and lying to myself. I was no Buddhist – nor could I pretend being one. I was past the spell cast by the fascinating intellectual construction which is Buddhism. I could no longer go back there. I no longer believed in the reality of that philosophy. In fact, in all honesty, I had never really believed in it. At first I had been entranced by its exoticism. Then I had discovered ever more profound levels of an esoteric doctrine I was proud of being able to comprehend, while they were ungraspable to most of the others. Taking all my common geese for immaculate swans, I had been self-absorbedly gratified, my vanity tickled pink by the intellectual performances that I thought I must have been capable of, since I was, or I thought I was, able to decipher the subtle arguments of the Mahayāna schools. However, after traveling through Asia, along with my spiritual coming-of-age, the elegant philosophical system of Buddhism had been debunked. I had remained sensitive to its poetical dimension, but I could no longer take its glib, Gnostic-like ontological and gnoseological assumptions seriously. Besides, I had met something far more wonderful: Fanya's eyes. She had opened up another world for me.

So, eventually, I also gave up *Sūnyāta*.

14

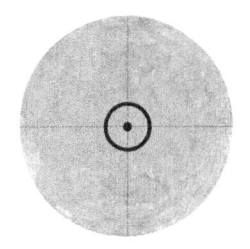

ILLUMINATIO.
THE BOOK OF THINGS MYSTERIOUS

At long last, I realized I could not carry out this impossible task, which I had taken upon myself out of pride, or in order to fill a void, or both. The book was truly beyond words, informulable. I finally understood that such an object could not exist. It would have been monstrous; its very existence would have abolished the world. For a long time I contemplated the implications of this fact. I spent months thinking of this delusion. Anyway, that's what I had been doing for years, for that matter, or maybe decades I had lost count of, for any other thought had long become impossible. Indeed, how could I have presumed to conceive the unconceivable? I understood I had chased a chimaera. One more. The last one.

But neither was I able to do or think of anything else. I was lost. I felt that my life had come to an end. I understood I had reached the end of the road – of all roads. Here I was, somewhere beyond regret, on the borderline between absolute unhappiness and the negligible, yet dogged, hope for an impossible miracle. I began to pray – not like before, timidly, half-heartedly, with no conviction, almost conventionally, but deeply, desperately, with tears, for days on end. And one Saturday night, when the dreary November rain was drizzling on the bare black boughs of the forlorn nut tree in the yard, and the harsh late autumn wind was shaking down the remaining nuts, which popped with crackling noises like shriveled, quavering castanets, onto the undersized grey stone ziggurat of the barren fountain and on the rusty plate roof of the long-neglected garage, the miracle occurred.

Anaesthetized by pain, curled up in my room – the same one where Fanya used to pray, long ago, surrounded by large icons of gold and purple – I was looking intensely into the flame of the silver oil lamp that was barely flickering under the icon of the Mother of God, the Unburnt Bush. In the wavering light, which was casting uncertain geometries on the walls, the Virgin's delicate face, framed by a red and green octagon on a golden background, suddenly seemed to be looking at me with Photini's eyes. At that moment I saw how the air began to shine. The room seemed to turn into a globe of golden crystal, like an aquarium filled with liquid, or maybe crystallized, light (*the light there almost solid*, my almost forgotten literary memory would have promptly supplied the proximal quote, if literature, at that moment, hadn't remained but a derisory crutch), which glided ever faster, defying gravitation, upwards on an invisible inclined plane. The walls seemed to dissolve into the light which rose from above, and kept growing until it became like the sun at noon. And at the centre of this effulgent radiance was myself, my very own person, that I seemed to contemplate from the outside.

Filled with an unspeakable joy, I perceived with my mind's eyes how the resplendent light permeated my entire body, how the brightness became united with my flesh and viscera, metamorphosing them into flame and light in their turn, just as incandescent metal becomes fire. Invaded by the light of grace, I lost all perception of the materiality and contours of my own body.

By some photosomatic phenomenon defying description, my body was turned into an active receptacle of transcendence. The opacity of matter gave way to the luminous transparency of the Holy Spirit, as human flesh was permeated by the glory of the Godhead, acquiring a new, transfigured corporality. The veil had been rent. I saw myself translucent, spiritually incorporated into the divine light which was pervading me, under the power of the blazing energy of grace. I had become fire.

I finally understood that which was obvious, and yet remained forever puzzling: that everything was a mystery. Not one, but *all* the things of the world were "Zahirs," secret theophanies, visible yet mysterious signs of God's presence and action. They were His thoughts, brought into existence out of love.

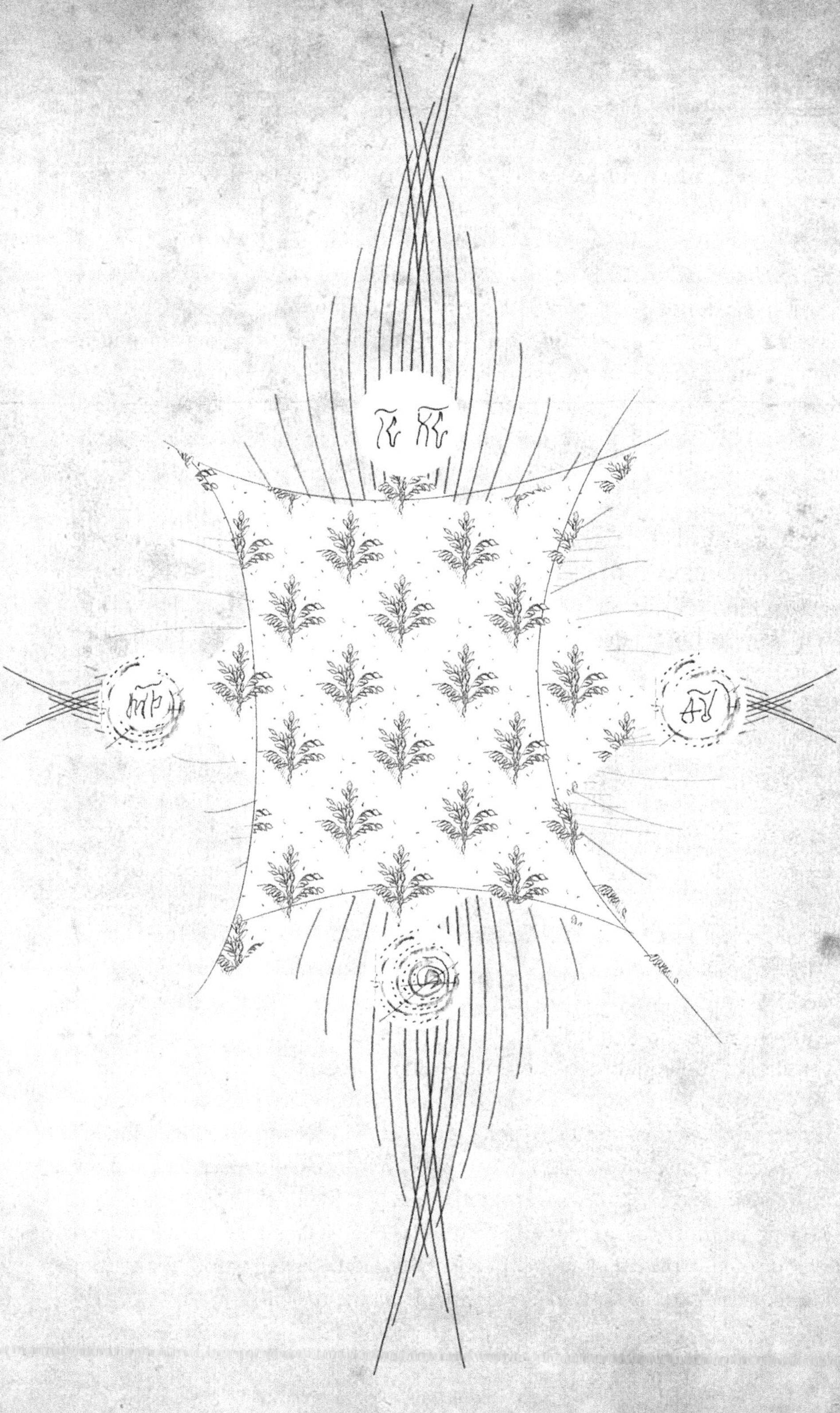
IC XC
MP

They were all mysteries; my own existence was an amazing mystery. United with Him, I understood that, out of a never-ending love (only now I understood that I had never been aware of this overwhelming love), God had heard my prayer, and He was making me, then and there, on the spot, co-author to the creation of the world. I understood that which I had read without comprehending, that for the divine providence, making the world, and keeping it in existence, are synonymous actions. Being beyond space, above time and the succession of aeons, God was creating and recreating the universe at every moment, eternally. And now He was making me – the unworthy, insignificant mite, the last grain of dust in this universe – part of His grandiose creation. By His will, I was witnessing the genesis of galaxies which once, at the beginning of creation, at the vertiginous moment which for the Creator was tantamount to an eternal Now, He had taken out of nothingness, bringing them into being from His own will. And I, the infinitesimal creature, made however in the divine image, had become, by His gift, a co-creator of this infinite miracle. I understood, with an understanding beyond my ken, that the impossible hypertext which I had wanted to write, *The Book of Things Unknown*, was the world itself, the very creation – an unpronounceable Book of Things Mysterious.

For everything was truly a mystery. Every atom of every wave, and of every cloud mirrored in the wave, every snowflake and every lightning, every leaf in every forest on the planet, every sea and every waterfall, with every drop in them and every photon of every ray of light refracted in it in rainbow iridescences, every single one of its billions of inhabitants – a unique person, kneaded in the image and likeness of this extraordinary God with Whom I myself was now united, Who had made me a close friend, a witness and a partner to the miracle of Creation – was an unrepeatable mystery. Mysteries were the supernovas and stellar systems of a cosmos that I was now contemplating, bedazzled; mysteries – the laws governing it; mysteries – the continents and equations; mysteries – all our lives, thoughts and destinies; mysteries – all the words ever spoken, all our caresses and steps, our gestures and questions, our births and deaths, encounters and passages, objects and beings, our choices and unbearable sufferances, our whispers and our impossible loves. Mysteries were all the sunsets, all our evanescent faces and fleeting memories, instants and centuries, our wishes and all our prayers ever uttered. How could all the things in this God-created world be anything but mysteries, along with their inscrutable divine reasons?

I saw, in the intelligible Light who was speaking to me in unwords, in a "language of states," that their apparent conspicuousness itself, their mere existence, which we take for granted, was the greatest mystery of all: the fact that He, the Creator, had made the world, with its infinitely complex operation, in such a way that it could appear to us banal, limpid and transparent; that we could even disregard Him, and view this amazing world, with an immense pride, as existing autonomously. The entire human history now appeared to me in unconceivable simultaneity, and I could see that everything in it was mysteriously guided by unseen Providence. I understood the supreme mystery of God's incarnation in this history, and I shuddered realizing that until then I had understood nothing whatsoever.

I knew that after this revelation, for which I had been brought into this world, I could die joyfully, to be definitively united with Him Who had made this gift to me (and Who had been waiting for me in the dense, dazzling, burning light...), the highest that can be given to any man. But this end was not yet allowed to me.

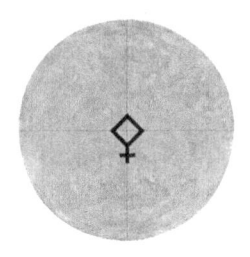

EPILOGUE

A week later I received a letter from Photini. I knew I would receive it, and already before opening it, I knew its content, just as I was now aware of many other things I had never even glimpsed before:

My dear,

All these years I have known how difficult it has been for you. I have also known that you have understood and forgiven me for the pain I have caused you, without wanting it. You know I couldn't have done otherwise without lying to myself, to you, and to God. I was happy in the seven years I spent with you, and I thank you. But in the end I had no doubt that, after all, my calling was to another kind of life, dedicated to Him. Even now, as I write these lines to you, God is watching over my shoulder, and He is my witness that I am absolutely sincere. You are the one I chose to wed, i.e. to be united with through the sacrament of marriage, I loved you, and the woman that I am still loves you, and always shall. What has changed is only the nature of that love, without human passion, but trying to contemplate the face of Christ in you. And now you also know that this is true: the closer you are to Him, the closer you get to the other people. And the more you know of God's love, the more grows in you the love for them.

I know that, Saturday night, you went through the hardest moment of your life. It was during the night vigil that I felt your dismay. The Six Psalms of the Last Judgement were being read, and perhaps an angel whispered to me that you needed help more than ever. So I prayed for you more than ever. I also knew that my prayer was heard, and that you received the gift for which I prayed. I saw your 'transfiguration,' I understood that was why it all happened, and why God had chosen you for me: not for the one you were, but for the one that you were to become.

He often does that, you know. I've come to get used to these ulterior motivations, which we can't understand on the spot, because we don't know the future. But He does. That's why, for Him, the future can be – and, very often, is – a cause of the present. I have been given a glimpse of this strange kind of circular, reverse causality, which seems to cross a fifth dimension, other than those of our world.

So I give glory to God that He dispensed for me to be His instrument in His plan with you.

Finally, I have understood that you had that destiny, that mission, in order to give witness about it, and I am waiting for it, as a last message from you in this world. I know, as I have always known, that we shall see each other again, there, in the unwaning light of the thrice-luminous Sun, a foretaste of which I saw that has been given to you.

Your sister in Christ,

Photini

*

But I didn't write the requested account immediately. After it hovered for a few months over the uncertain border between language and the unnamable, eventually its words were given to me in a dream the colour of gold,

The Book of Things Unknown

purple, and emerald, from which I woke up, one white February morning, feeling it was very warm, and having in my mouth and nostrils a distinct, persistent taste of sea salt.

Dear Photini,

As you know, I have always been fascinated by libraries... ✣

THE INTERTEXTUAL ALLUSIONS, REFERENCES, OR QUOTES IN THE TEXT INCLUDE:

Gerard *Genette, Palimpsestes: La littérature au second degré* (Seuil, 1982), for a definition of the literary phenomenon of hypertextuality: *"Hypertextualité: j'entends par là toute relation unissant un texte B (que j'appellerai hypertexte) à un texte antérieur A (que j'appellerai, bien sûr, hypotexte) sur lequel il se greffe d'une manière qui n'est pas celle du commentaire."* If we consider Borges' "The Zahir" as the reference text A or 'hypotext' (in the sense given by Genette), then the story above is one of its possible texts B or 'hypertexts.'

Moartea şi busola. Proză completă 1 (Jorge Luis Borges, translation and notes by Irina Dogaru, Cristina Haulica, Andrei Ionescu, editor, foreword and presentations by Andrei Ionescu, Polirom, 2005; *Cartea de nisip. Proză completă 2* (J. L. Borges, translation and notes by Cristina Haulica and Andrei Ionescu, editor and presentations by Andrei Ionescu, Polirom, 2006; Poezii (J. L. Borges, translation and preface by Andrei Ionescu, Polirom, 2005).

Saint Bonaventura, *Itinerarium mentis in Deum* (*The Journey of the Mind Into God*), introduction, translation, commentary by Philotheus Boehner, Franciscan Institute, Saint Bonaventure University, New York, 1956: *The Triple Way*, or *Love Enkindled* (*in Writings on the Spiritual Life. Works of St. Bonaventure*, Vol. X, ed. E. Coughlin, 2006, after *De triplici via, alias Incendium amoris* (initial title *Itinerarium mentis in se ipsum*), in *S. Bonaventurae Opera omnia*, Quarachi, 1882-1902, VIII).

Chāndogya Upanishad, Bṛihadāraṇyaka Upanishad, and *The Saundaryalaharī, or Flood of Beauty*, traditionally ascribed to Śaṅkarācārya (translated by Norman Brown, Harvard Univ. Press, 1958); *Spaţiul eteric la Eminescu* (A. Dirlau, in *Convorbiri literare*, Oct. 1988), for *akasha*, the etheric space.

N. Bland, *Account of the Atesh Kedah, a Biographical Work on the Persian Poets, by Hajji Lutf Ali Beg, of Ispakan* (Journal of the Royal Asiatic Society of Great Britain and Ireland, Vol. 7, no. 2 /1843, Cambridge University Press), for Lutf Ali and his *Temple of Fire*.

REFERENCES

The Cambridge Companion to Jorge Luis Borges (ed. Edwin Williamson), and Hellmut Ritter, *The Ocean of the Soul. Men, the World and God in the Stories of Farīdal-Dīn 'Aṭṭār* (transl. John O'Kane, Brill 2003), for 'Aṭṭār of Nishapur, *Asrār nāma*, and the *Batin–Zahir* pair.

Alexandra David-Neel and Lama Yongden, *Secret Oral Teachings in Tibetan Buddhist Sects*, transl. M. Hardy, City Lights Books, 1967, for the *Prājñapāramita* and the doctrine of interdependent origins.

The Chinese Classics, Vol. V: *The Chu'n Ts'ew, with The Tso Chuen*. Translation, critical and exegetical notes, prolegomena by James Legge, London Missionary Society. Hong Kong: Lane, Crawford & Co. London: Trubner & Co., 60 Paternoster Row, 1872. Reprinted in China, 1939.

The Decision of the Chalcedon Fourth Ecumenical Synod, on the two natures of Christ.

Ioan Petru Culianu's short stories collected under the title *The Diaphanous Scroll* (particularly *Miss Emeralds, The Last Appearance of Alicia H.*, and *The Enigma of the Emerald Disc*), for the twin *topoi* of the taste of sea salt connected to the feminine character having no articulations like the angels.

Michael Gibbs, *All or nothing. An anthology of blank books* (RGAP, Cromford, 2005) and Craig Douglas Dworkin, *No Medium* (MIT Press, Cambridge, MA, 2013), for the unexpectedly lush blank-book subgenre.

Saint John of the Cross, *The Dark Night of the Soul,* translated by Kieran Kavanaugh and Otilio Rodriguez, ICS Publications, 1991.

Ezra Pound, *The Cantos*, Faber & Faber, London, 1975, for the lines about love (Canto LXXXI), and the solid light (Canto XCIII).

Saint Niketas Stethatos, *Life of Saint Symeon the New Theologian*, quoted in Nichifor Crainic, *Sanctity – the Fulfilment of the Human. A Course in Mystical Theology 1935-1936,* for the experience of the transfiguration of Saint Symeon's body, ecstatically transformed into light.

Mircea Cartarescu, *Blinding*, translated by Sean Cotter, Archipelago Books, 2013.

Elias Canetti, *Auto-da-Fé*, transl. C. V. Wedgwood: New York, Continuum, 1981.

AUTHOR'S NOTES ON ILLUSTRATIONS

The Book of Things Unknown is fiction, not a theological paper, and the function fulfilled by the symbol at each chapter heading is poetical-metaphorical, literary and fictional. I take my materials from different registers, as literature often does, in order to achieve certain literary effects – mystery in this case.

Many of the planet or asteroid symbols used as chapter headings were named after Greek or Roman mythological figures and are still used as shorthand by astronomers in scientific writing. Their function here is emphatically not occult. I chose them because I liked their names and found them both poetic and coherent with the respective chapters.

Mercury, Mars, Saturn, and Neptune are planets in our solar system, plus the Sun. Lunar Node North and the Lot of Divinity are mathematically calculated points in space. Ariadne, Babel, Vesta, Flora, Minos, Acacia, Abstracta, Pallas are asteroids.

SYMBOLS ON CHAPTER HEADINGS

CHAPTER	TITLE	PLANET/ASTEROID
Chapter 1	The Library	Ariadne
	The mythical Ariadne shows Theseus the way through the labyrinth, being suitable for Chapter 1.	
Chapter 2	Hypertext	Babel
	What better symbol for the "libraries" in Chapter 2 than "Babel" (alluding to the short story, "The Library of Babel" by Borges)?	
Chapter 3	Fanya	Vesta
	Vesta was a goddess of the hearth, home and marriage.	

AUTHOR'S NOTES ON ILLUSTRATIONS

Chapter 4	Fahrenheit '89	Mars	♂

Mars governs war, being appropriate for the violent revolution.

Chapter 5	*Florigera Rosis Halo*	Flora	⚶

Flora aligns with "Florigera rosis halo" and paradise.

Chapter 6	Photini	Saturn	♄

Saturn is said to govern ascetic life, including nuns, monks and hermits.

Chapter 7	'Aṭṭār	Minos	⌇

King Minos built the Cretan labyrinth, so he is in charge of the Timisoara labyrinth.

Chapter 8	The Book About the Qilin	Acacia	☿

The Greek word *akakios* means "innocent, not evil," it also renders the Hebrew word *shittah*, the Biblical tree from whose wood the tabernacle was made. Acacia stands for innocence, purity, to be protected, virginity, tree of life, resurrection. It could also have presided over chapters 1 or 3, but it got chapter 8 since it's consistent with the attributes of the fabulous Qilin.

Chapter 9	Zahir	Lot of Divinity	☉

The lot of divinity (also called pars *solis* – part of the sun, *pars spiriti* – lot of spirit, *pars futurorum* – part of things to come) is a mathematically calculated astronomical point, signifying concerns of the mind, intellect, spirit and soul. Mentioned by the ancient geographer-mathematician Ptolemy and used scientifically by Byzantine Greeks, Arabs and Western Europeans.

Chapter 10   The Book of Things Unknown   Lunar Node North   ☊

Lunar Node North is the lesson to be learnt – in this case, The Book of Things Unknown.

Chapter 11   The Book of Things Unintelligible   Mercury   ☿

Mercury is of course Hermetic, so it represents Chapter 11.

Chapter 12   The Book of Things Invisible   Abstracta

Abstracta goes well with apophatism and blank books.

Chapter 13   The Book of Things Ignored   Neptune   ♆

Hazy Neptune presides over Buddhism.

Chapter 14   *Illuminatio*. The Book of Things Mysterious   Sun   ☉

This chapter is immersed in light, a sui-generis theosis. The Fathers generally apply the title of "Sun of Righteousness" to Christ.

Epilogue   Pallas   ⚴

Pallas is wisdom – in this case, Photini's God-granted wisdom.

Notes on Selected Drawings

Chapter 1   The Library

The Chinese characters on the labyrinth of books are three different synonyms for maze or labyrinth, with nuances of meandering or lost.

Chapter 2   Hypertext

Tower of Babel. Chinese characters mean "library" in ancient script.

Chapter 3   Fanya

Steph Fania = Stephany + Epiphany. The words on the rose are from the Romanian text.

Chapter 6   Photini

Greek letters NI KA = Victory. Romanian words to the left of the figure: *jertfă vie binecuvântată* meaning "blessed living sacrifice/oblation."

Chapter 7   'Aṭṭār

On the spines of the many small books around the rim of the image *Palimpsest Altar* is written: *Cartea lucrurilor neștiute* (The Book of Things Unknown).

Chapter 9   Zahir

Words around Sufi image: Zahir, Batin, Batinyya.

Chapter 13   The Book of Things Ignored

The astronomical symbol in the center of the image is Neptune's trident. Again, "hazy Neptune presides over Buddhism."

Chapter 14   *Illuminatio.* The Book of Things Mysterious

Image inspired by the Icon of the Theotokos, the Unburnt Bush.

Top abbreviation: ICXC (First and last letters in Greek for IHCOYC XPICTOC, *Jesus Christ*)

Left side: MP (Greek for *Mater Theos*: The Mother of God)

Right side: A'Ω (Greek *Alpha/Omega*: First and last letters of the Greek alphabet, representing Christ/God in the Book of Revelation.

Inside Back Cover Illustration   This final drawing is a variant of the tonsure. The words are taken from the text of Chapters 5 and 6 respectively:

I'll be always praying for you... farther ever further...more slowly... my soul unsoothed with a longing...

EARTH   HORIZON

SLAVA (GLORY)

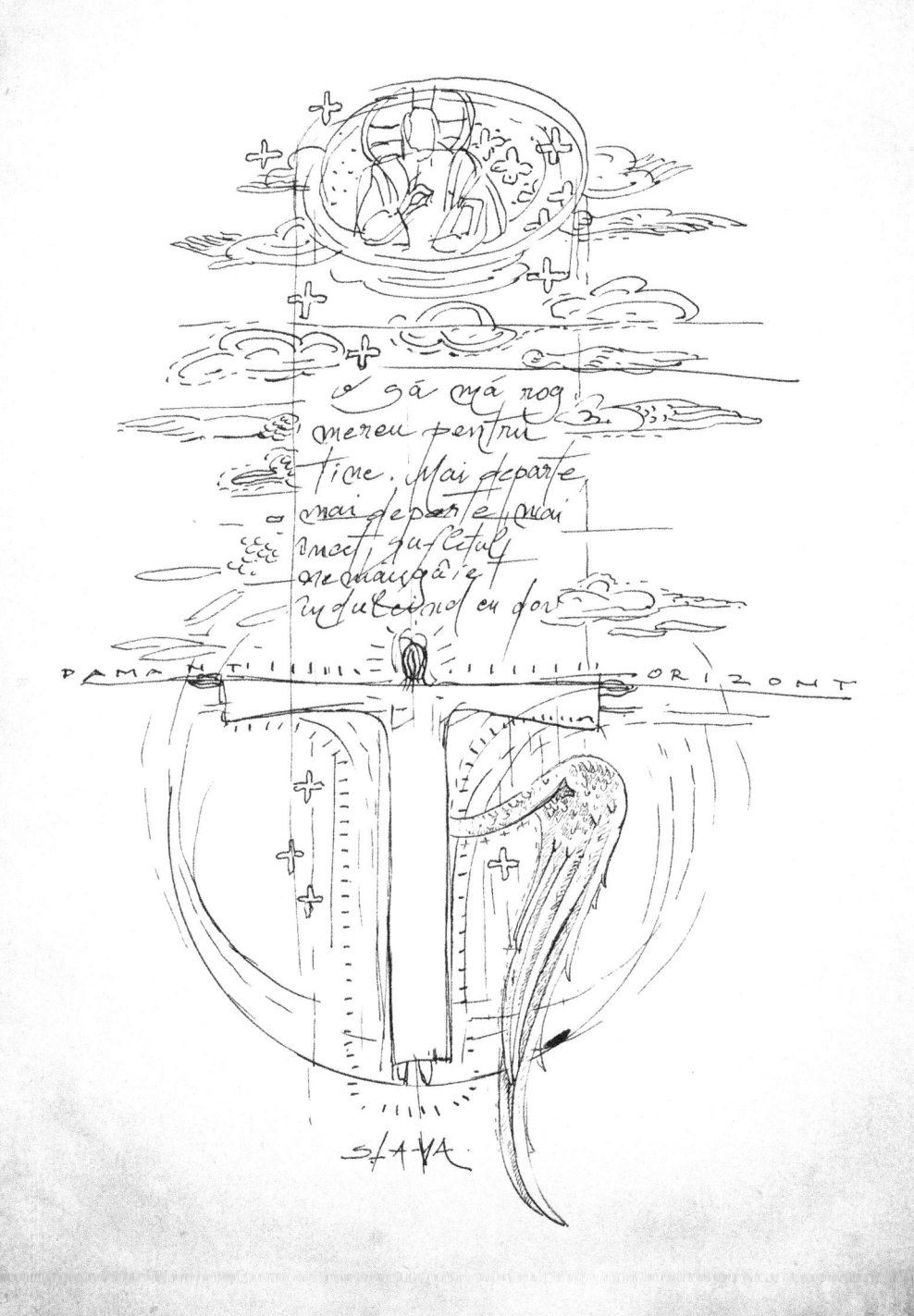

o să mă rog
mereu pentru
tine. Mai departe
mai departe, mai
încet, sufletul
ne mângâie
îndulcind cu dor

PAMANT   ORIZONT

SLAVA

ABOUT THE AUTHOR

An admirer of Dante, Pound, Blake, Rilke, Eminescu, a spiritual traveler in a less known Asia, PhD in the history of religions (author of a large transdisciplinary study on Confucianism and Christianity titled *The China of Grace*), a translator of H.T. Engelhardt's book *After God*, a practicing Orthodox Christian, close to the Orthodox monastic environment, the Romanian author Andrei Dîrlău, in *The Book of Things Unknown* proposes a rewriting in a mystical key of Borges' story "The Zahir" transposed into an imaginary expanse imbued with curious and exceptional references.